Edmund Hodgson Yates

Land at Last

Vol. 1

Edmund Hodgson Yates

Land at Last
Vol. 1

ISBN/EAN: 9783337258238

Printed in Europe, USA, Canada, Australia, Japan

Cover: Foto ©Andreas Hilbeck / pixelio.de

More available books at **www.hansebooks.com**

A Novel

IN THREE BOOKS.

BY

EDMUND YATES,

AUTHOR OF "BROKEN TO HARNESS," "RUNNING THE GAUNTLET,"
ETC.

"Post tenebras lux."

BOOK I.—Making for Shore.

LONDON:

CHAPMAN AND HALL, 193 PICCADILLY.

MDCCCLXVI.

CONTENTS OF BOOK I.

LAND AT LAST.

𝕭ook the 𝕱irst.

CHAPTER I.

IN THE STREETS.

IT was between nine and ten o'clock on a January night, and the London streets were in a state of slush. During the previous night snow had fallen heavily, and the respectable portion of the community, which, according to regular custom, had retired to bed at eleven o'clock, had been astonished, on peering out from behind a corner of the window-curtain when they arose, to find the roads and the neighbouring housetops covered with a thick white incrustation. The pavements were already showing dank dabs of footmarks, which even the snow then falling failed to fill up; and the roadway speedily lost its winter-garment and became sticky with congealed mud. Then the snow ceased, and a sickly straggling bit of winter-sunlight, a mere parody on the real thing, half light and half warmth, came lurking out between the dun clouds; and under its influence the black-specked covering of the roofs melted, and the water-pipes ran with cold black liquid filth. The pavement had given it up long ago, and resumed its normal winter state of sticky slippery grease—grease which clung to the boots and roused the wildest rage of foot-passengers by causing them to slip backward when they wanted to make progress, and which accumulated in the direst manner on the landing-places and street-corners,—the first bits of refuge after the perils of the crossing,—where it heaped itself in aggravating lumps and shiny rings under the heels of foot-passengers just arrived, having been shaken and stamped off the soles of passengers who had just preceded them. So it had continued all day; but towards the afternoon the air had grown colder, and a whisper had run round that it froze again. Cutlers who had been gazing with a melancholy air on the placards "Skates" in their window, and had determined on removing them, as a bad joke against themselves, decided on letting them remain. Boys who had been delighted in the morning at the sight of the snow, and proportionately chopfallen towards middle-day at the sight of the thaw, had plucked up again and seen visions of snowballing matches, slides on the gutters, and, most delicious of all, omnibus-horses both down at once on the slippery road. Homeward-bound City-clerks, their day's work over, shivered in the omnibuses, and told each other how they were afraid it had come at last, and reminded each other of what the newspapers had said about the flocks of wild-geese and other signs of a hard winter, and moaned lugubriously about the advanced price of coals and the difficulties of locomotion certain to be consequent on the frost.

But when the cruel black night had set regularly in, a dim sleek soft drizzle began to fall, and all hopes or fears of frost were at an end. Slowly

and gently it came down, wrapping the streets as
with a damp pall; stealing quietly in under umbrellas; eating its way through the thickest broad-
cloth, matting the hair and hanging in dank, un-
wholesome beads on the beards of all unlucky
enough to be exposed to it.   It meant mischief,
this drizzle, and it carried out its intention.   Om-
nibus-drivers and cabmen knew it at once from
long experience, donned their heavy tarpaulin-
capes, and made up their minds for the worst.
The professional beggars knew it too.   The pave-
ment-chalking tramp, who had selected a tolerably
dry spot under the lee of a wall, no sooner felt its
first damp breath than he blew out his paper-
lantern, put the candle into his pocket, stamped
out as much of the mackerel and the ship at sea
as he had already stencilled, and made off.   The
man in the exemplary shirt-collar and apron, who
had planted himself before the chemist's window
to procure an extra death-tinge from the light re-
flected from the blue bottle, packed up his linen
and decamped, fearing lest his stock-in-trade—
his virtue and his lucifers—might be injured by

damp. The brass bands which had been playing outside the public-houses shouldered their instruments and went inside; the vendors of second-hand books covered their openly-displayed stock with strips of baize and dismissed their watchful boys, conscious that no petty thief would risk the weather for so small a prey. The hot-potato men blew fiercer jets of steam out of their tin kitchens, as though calling on the public to defy dull care and comfort themselves with an antidote to the general wretchedness; and the policemen stamped solemnly and slowly round their beats, as men impressed with the full knowledge that, as there was not the remotest chance of their being relieved from their miserable fate until the morning, they might as well bear themselves with as much dignity as possible under the circumstances.

It was bad every where; but in no place at the West-end of London was it so bad as at the Regent Circus. There the great tide of humanity had been ebbing and flowing all day; there hapless females in shoals had struggled across the roaring sea of Oxford Street, some conveyed by the crossing-sweeper, some drifting helplessly under the poles of omnibuses and the wheels of hansom cabs. There the umbrellas of the expectant omnibus-seekers jostled each other with extra virulence; and there the edges of the pavements were thick with dark alluvial deposits kicked hither and thither by the feet of thousands. All day there had been a bustle and a roar round this spot; and at ten o'clock at night it had but little diminished. Omnibus-conductors, like kites and vultures, clawed and wrangled over the bodies of their victims, who in a miserable little flock huddled together in a corner, and dashed out helplessly and without purpose as each lumbering vehicle drew up. Intermingled with these were several vagabond boys, whose animal spirits no amount of wet or misery could quell, and who constituted themselves a kind of vedette or outpost-guard, giving warning of the approach of the different omnibuses in much pleasantly familiar speech, "Now, guv'nor, for Bayswater! Hatlas comin' up! Ready now for Nottin' 'Ill!'"

At the back of the little crowd, sheltering herself under the lee of the houses, stood a slight
female figure, a mere slight slip of a girl, dressed
only in a clinging gown and a miserable tightly-
drawn shawl. Her worn bonnet was pulled over
her face, her arms were clasped before her, and
she stood in a doorway almost motionless. The
policeman tramping leisurely by had at first imagined her to be an omnibus-passenger waiting
for a vehicle; but some twenty minutes after he
had first noticed her, finding her still in the same
position, he took advantage of a pretended trial of
the security of various street-doors to scrutinise
her appearance. To the man versed in such
matters the miserable garb told its own tale—
its wearer was a pauper; and a beggar the man
in office surmised, although the girl had made no
plaint, had uttered no word, had remained im-
movable and statue-like, gazing blankly before
her. The policeman had been long enough in
the force to know that the girl's presence in the
doorway was an offence in the eyes of the law;
but he was a kindly-hearted Somersetshire man,

and he performed his duty in as pleasant a way
as he could, by gently pulling a corner of the
drabbled shawl, and saying, "You mustn't stand
here, lass; you must move on, please." The
shawl-wearer never looked up or spoke, but shivering slightly, stepped out into the dank mist,
and floated, phantom-like, across the road.

Gliding up the upper part of Regent Street,
keeping close to the houses, and walking with her
head bent down and her arms always folded tightly
across her breast, she struck off into a bystreet to
the right, and, crossing Oxford Market, seemed
hesitating which way to turn. For an instant
she stopped before the window of an eating-house,
where thick columns of steam were yet playing
round the attenuated remains of joints, or cast-
ing a greasy halo round slabs of pudding. As
the girl gazed at these wretched remnants of a
wretched feast, she raised her head, her eyes
glistened, her pinched nostrils dilated, and for
an instant her breath came thick and fast; then,
drawing her shawl more tightly round her, and
bending her head to avoid as much as possible

the rain, which came thickly scudding on the rising wind, she hurried on, and only stopped for shelter under the outstretched blind of a little chandler's shop—a wretched shelter, for the blind was soaked through, and the rain dripped from it in little pools, and the wind shook it in its frame, and eddied underneath it with a wet and gusty whirl; but there was something of comfort to the girl in the warm look of the gaslit shop, in the smug rotund appearance of the chandler, in the distant glimmer of the fire on the glazed door of the parlour at the back. Staring vacantly before him while mechanically patting a conical lump of lard, not unlike the bald cranium of an elderly gentleman, the chandler became aware of the girl's face at the window; and seeing Want legibly inscribed by Nature's never-erring hand on every feature of that face, and being a humane man, he was groping in the till for some small coin to bestow in charity, when from the back room came a sharp shrill voice, " Jim, time to shut up !" and at the sound of the voice the chandler hastily retreated, and, a small boy suddenly appearing, pulled up the overhanging blind, and having lost its shelter, the girl set forth again.

But her course was nearly at an end. To avoid a troop of boys who, arm-in-arm, came breasting up the street singing the burden of a negro-song, she turned off again into the main thoroughfare, and had barely gained the broad shadow of the sharp-steepled church in Langham Place, when she felt her legs sinking under her, her brain reeling, her heart throbbing in her breast like a ball of fire. She tottered and clung to the church-railing for support. In the next instant she was surrounded by a little crowd, in which she had a vision of painted faces and glistening silks, a dream of faint words of commiseration overborne by mocking laughter and ribald oaths, oaths made more fearful still by being uttered in foreign accents, of bitter jests and broad hints of drunkenness and shame; finally, of the strident voice of the policeman telling her again to "move on!" The dead faintness, consequent on cold and wet and weariness and starvation, passed away for the time, and she obeyed the mandate. Passively she crept away a few steps up a deserted bystreet until her tormentors had left her quite alone; then she sunk down, shivering, on a door-step, and burying her face in her tattered shawl, felt that her end was come.

There she remained, the dead damp cold striking through her lower limbs and chilling them to stone, while her head was one blazing fire. Gradually her limbs became numbed and lost to all sensation, a sickening empty pain was round her heart, a dead apathy settling down over her mind and brain. The tramping of feet was close upon her, the noise of loud voices, the ringing shouts of loud laughter, were in her ears; but she never raised her head from the tattered shawl, nor by speech or motion did she give the smallest sign of life. Men passed her constantly, all making for one goal, the portico next to that in which she had sunk down helpless—men with kindly hearts attuned to charity, who, had they known the state of the wretched wayfarer, would have exerted themselves bravely in her succour, but whom a London life had so inured to spectacles of casual misery and vice, that a few only cast a passing glance on the stricken woman and passed on. They came singly and in twos and threes; but none spoke to her, none noticed her save by a glance and a shoulder-shrug.

Then, as the icy hands of Cold and Want gradually stealing over her seemed to settle round the region of her heart, the girl gave one low faint cry, "God help me! it's come at last—God help me!" and fell back in a dead swoon.

CHAPTER II.

THE house to which all the jovial fellows who passed the girl on the doorstep with such carelessness were wending their way was almost unique in the metropolis. The rumour ran that it had originally been designed for stables, and indeed there was a certain mews-ish appearance about its architectural elevation; it had the squat, squabby, square look of those buildings from whose upper-floors clothes-lines stretch diagonally across stable-yards; and you were at first surprised at finding an imposing portico with an imposing bell in a position where you looked for the folding-doors of a coach-house. Whether there had been any truth in the report or not, it is certain that the owner of the property speedily saw his way to more money than he could have gained by the ignoble pursuit of stabling horses, and made alterations in his building which converted it into several sets of spacious, roomy, and comfortable, if not elegant chambers. The upper rooms were duly let, and speedily became famous—thus-wise. When Parmegiano Wilkins made his first great success with his picture of " Boadicea at Breakfast,"—connoisseurs and art-critics will recollect the marvellous manner in which the chip in the porridge of the Queen of the Iceni was rendered,—Mr. Caniche, the great picture-dealer, to whom Wilkins had mortgaged himself body and soul for three years, felt it neces-sary that his next works should be submitted to the private inspection of the newspaper-writers and the *cognoscenti* previous to their going into the Academy Exhibition. On receiving a letter to this effect from Caniche, Wilkins was at his wits' end. He was living, for privacy's sake, in a little cot-tage on the outskirts of Epping Forest, and having made a success, had naturally alienated all his friends whose rooms in town would otherwise have been available for the display of his pictures; he thought— and there the astute picture-dealer agreed

with him—that it would be unwise to send them to
Caniche's shop (it was before such places were
called "galleries"), as tending to make public the
connection between them; and Wilkins did not
know what to do. Then Caniche came to his
rescue. Little Jimmy Dabb, who had been Gold-
Medallist and Travelling-Student at the Academy
three years beforehand, and who, for sheer sake
of bread-winning, had settled down as one of
Caniche's labourers, had a big studio in the stable-
like edifice near Langham Church. In it he painted
those bits of domestic life,—dying children on beds,
weeping mothers, small table with cut-orange, Bible
and physic by bedside, and pitying angel dimly
hovering between mantelpiece and ceiling,—which,
originally in oil, and subsequently in engravings,
had such a vast sale, and brought so much ready
money to Caniche's exchequer. The situation was
central; why not utilise it? No sooner thought of
than done : a red cotton-velvet coverlet was spread
over Jimmy Dabb's bed in the corner; a Dutch
carpet, red with black flecks, was, at Caniche's
expense, spread over the floor, paint-smeared and

burnt with tobacco-ash; two gorgeous easels, on
which were displayed Wilkins' two pictures, "The
Bird in the Hand"—every feather in the bird and
the dirt in the nails of the ploughboy's hand mar-
vellously delineated—and "Crumbs of Comfort,"
each crumb separate, and the loaf in the background so real, that the Dowager-Countess of
Rundall, a celebrated household manager, declared
it at once to be a "slack-baked quartern." Invita-
tion-cards, wonderfully illuminated in Old-English
characters, and utterly illegible, were sent forth
to rank, fashion, and talent, who duly attended.
Crowds of gay carriages choked up the little
street: Dabb in his Sunday-clothes did the honours;
Caniche, bland, smiling, and polyglot, flitted here
and there, his clerk took down orders for proof-
copies, and the fortune of the chambers was made.
They were so original, so artistic, so convenient,
they were just the place for a painter. Smudge,
R.A., who painted portraits of the aristocracy, who
wore a velvet-coat, and whose name was seen in
the tail-end of the list of fashionables at evening-
parties, took a vacant set at once; and Clement

Walkinshaw of the Foreign Office, who passed such spare time as his country could afford him in illuminating missals, in preparing designs for stained glass, and in hanging about art-circles generally, secured the remainder of the upper-floor, and converted it into a Wardour-Street Paradise, with hanging velvet *portières*, old oak cabinets, Venetian glass, marqueterie tables, Sèvres china, escutcheons of armour, and Viennese porcelain pipes.

Meanwhile, utterly uncaring for and utterly independent of what went on upstairs, the denizens of the lower story kept quietly on. Who were the denizens of the lower story? who but the well-known Titian Sketching-Club! How many men, who, after struggling through Suffolk Street and the Portland Gallery, have won their way to fame and fortune, have made their *coup d'essai* on the walls of the chambers rented by the Titian Sketch-ing-Club! Outsiders, who professed great love for art, but who only knew the two or three exhibitions of the season, and only recognised the score of names in each vouchsafed for by the newspaper-

critics, would have been astonished to learn the
amount of canvas covered, pains taken, and skill
brought to bear upon the work of the members of
the Titian. There are guilds, and companies of
Freemasons, and brotherhoods by the score in
London; but I know of none where the grand
spirit of Camaraderie is so carried out as in this.
It is the nearest thing to the *Vie de Bohème* of
Paris of Henri Murger that we can show; there
is more liberty of speech and thought and action,
less reticence, more friendship,—when friendship
is understood by purse-sharing, by sick-bedside-
watching, by absence of envy, jealousy, hatred,
and all uncharitableness,—more singleness of purpose, more contempt for shams and impostures and
the dismal fetters of conventionality, than in any
other circle of English society with which I am
acquainted.

It was a grand night with the Titians; no
model was carefully posed on the " throne" that
evening; no intelligent class was grouped round
on the rising benches, copying from the " draped"
or the " nude ;" none of the wardrobe or properties

of the club (and it is rich in both),—none of the
coats of mail or suits of armour, hauberks and
broadswords, buff boots, dinted breastplates, carved
ebony crucifixes, ivory-hafted daggers, Louis-Onze
caps, friars' gowns and rosaries, nor other portions
of the stock-in-trade, were on view. The "send-
ing-in" day for the approaching Exhibition of the
British Institution was at hand; and the dis-
coloured smoky old walls of the Titians, the rickety
easels piled round the room, all available ledges
and nooks, were covered with the works of the
members of the club, which they fully intended to
submit for exhibition. A very Babel, in a thick
fog of tobacco-smoke, through which loomed the
red face of Flexor the famous model, like the sun
in November, greeted you on your entrance.
Flexor pretended to take the hats, but the visitors
seemed to know him too well, and contented themselves with nodding at him in a friendly manner,
and retaining their property. Then you passed
into the rooms, where you found yourself wedged-
up amongst a crowd of perhaps the most extraor-
dinary-looking beings you ever encountered. Little

men with big heads and long beards, big men with bald heads and shaved cheeks, and enormous moustaches and glowering spectacles; tall thin straggling men, who seemed all profile, and whose full face you could never catch; dirty shaggy little men, with heads of hair like red mops, and no apparent faces underneath, whose eyes flashed through their elf-locks, and who were explaining their pictures with singular pantomimic power of their sinewy hands, and notably of their ever-flashing thumbs; moon-faced solemn didactic men, prosing away on their views of art to dreary discontented listeners; and foppish, smart little fellows, standing a-tiptoe to get particular lights, shading their eyes with their hands, and backing against the company generally. Moving here and there among the guests was the Titians' president, honest old Tom Wrigley, who had been " at it," as he used to say, for thirty years, without making any great mark in his profession, but who was cordially beloved for his kind-heartedness and *bonhomie*, and who had a word and a joke for all. As he elbowed his way through the room he spoke right and left.

"Hallo, Tom Rogers!—hallo, Tom! That's an improvement, Tom, my boy! Got rid of the heavy browns, eh? weren't good, those heavy browns; specially for a Venetian atmosphere, eh, Tom? Much better, this.—How are you, Jukes? Old story, Jukes?—hen and chickens, ducks in the pond, horse looking over the gate? Quite right, Jukes; stick to that, if it pays. Much better than the death of J. Cæsar on a twenty-foot canvas, which nobody would be fool enough to buy. Stick to the ducks, Jukes, old fellow.—What's the matter, George? Why so savage, my son?"

"Here's Scumble!" said the young man addressed, in an undertone.

"And what of that, George? Mr. Scumble is a Royal Academician, it is true; and consequently a mark for your scorn and hatred, George. But it's not *his* fault; he never did any thing to aspire to such a dignity. It's your British public, George, which is such an insensate jackass as to buy Scumble's pictures, and to tell him he's a genius."

"He was on the Hanging-Committee last year, and—"

"Ah, so he was; and your 'Aristides' was kicked out, and so was my 'Hope Deferred,' which was a deuced sight better than your big picture, Master George; but see how I shall treat him.—How do you do, Mr. Scumble? You're very welcome here, sir."

Mr. Scumble, R.A., who had a head like a tinloaf, and a face without any earthly expression, bowed his acknowledgments, and threw as much warmth into his manner as he possibly could, apparently labouring under a notion that he was marked out for speedy assassination. "This is indeed a char-ming collection! Great talent among the ri-sing men, Mr.—pardon me—President! This now, for instance,—a most charming landscape!"

"Yes, old boy; you may say that," said a square-built man smoking a clay-pipe, and leaning with his elbows on the easel on which the picture was placed. "I mean the real thing,—not this; which ain't bad though, is it? Not that I should say so; 'cause for why; which I did it!" and here the square-built man removed one of his elbows from the easel, and dug it into the sacred ribs of Scumble, R.A.

" Bad, sir !" said Scumble, recoiling from the thrust, and still with the notion of a secret dagger hidden behind the square-built man's waistcoat; " it's magnificent, superb, Mr.—!"

" Meaning me ? Potts !" said the square-built man—" Charley Potts, artist, U.E., or unsuccessful exhibitor at every daub-show in London. That's the Via Mala, that is. I was there last autumn with Geoffrey Ludlow and Tom Bleistift. 'Show me a finer view than that,' I said to those fellows, when it burst upon us. 'If you'd a Scotchman with you,' said Tom, 'he'd say it wasn't so fine as the approach to Edinburgh.' 'Would he?' said I. 'If he said any thing of that sort, I'd show him that view, and—and rub his nose in it!'"

Mr. Scumble, R.A., smiled in a sickly manner, bowed feebly, and passed on. Old Tom Wrigley laughed a great boisterous " Ha, ha !" and went on his way. Charley Potts remained before his picture, turning his back on it, and puffing out great volumes of smoke. He seemed to know every body in the room, and to be known to and greeted by most of them. Some slapped him on the back, some poked him in the ribs, others laid their forefingers alongside their noses and winked; but all called him "Charley," and all had some pleasant word for him; and to all he had something to say in return.

"Hallo, Fred Snitterfield!" he called out to a fat man in a suit of shepherd's-plaid dittoes. "Halloa, Fred! how's your brother Bill? What's he been doing? Not here to-night, of course?"

"No; he wasn't very well," said the man addressed. "He's got—"

"Yes, yes; I know, Fred!" said Charley Potts. "Wife won't let him! That's it, isn't it, old boy? He only dined out once in his life without leave, and then he sent home a telegram to say he was engaged; and when his wife received the telegram she would not believe it, because she said it wasn't his handwriting! Poor old Bill! Did he sell that 'Revenge' to what's-his-name—that Manchester man—Prebble?"

. "Lord, no! Haven't you heard? Prebble's

smashed up,— all his property gone to the devil!"

"Ah, then Prebble will find it again some day, no doubt. Look out! here's Bowie!"

Mr. Bowie was the art-critic of a great daily journal. In early life he had courted art himself; but lacking executive power, he had mixed up a few theories and quaint conceits which he had learned with a great deal of acrid bile, with which he had been gifted by nature, and wrote the most pungent and malevolent art-notices of the day. A tall, light-haired, vacant-looking man, like a light-house without any light in it, peering uncomfortably over his stiff white cravat, and fumbling nervously at his watch-chain. Clinging close to him, and pointing out to him various pictures as they passed them by, was quite another style of man,— Caniche, the great picture-dealer,—an under-sized lively Gascon, black-bearded from his chin, round which it was closely cut, to his beady black eyes, faultlessly dressed, sparkling in speech, affable in manner, at home with all.

"Ah, ah!" said he, stopping before the easel,

"the Via Mala! Not bad—not at all bad!" he continued, with scarcely a trace of a foreign accent. "Yours, Charley Potts? yours, *mon brave?* De-caidedly an improvement, Charley! You go on that way, mai boy, and some day—"

"Some day you'll give me twenty pound, and sell me for a hundred! won't you, Caniche?— generous buffalo!" growled Charley, over his pipe.

The men round laughed, but Caniche was not a bit offended. "Of course," he said, simply, "I will, indeed; that is my trade! And if you could find a man who would give you thirty, you would throw me over in what you call a brace of shakes! *N'est-ce pas?* Meanwhile find the man to give you thirty. He is not here; I mean coming now. —How do you do, Herr Stompff?"

Mr. Caniche (popularly known as Cannish among the artists) winced as he said this, for Herr Stompff was his great rival and bitterest enemy.

A short, bald-headed, gray-bearded man was Mr. Stompff,—a Hamburger,—who, on his first arrival in England, had been an importer of piping bullfinches at Hull; then a tobacconist in St. Mary

Axe; and who finally had taken up picture-selling,.
and did an enormous business. No one could tell.
that he was not an Englishman from his talk, and
an Englishman with a marvellous fluency in the.
vernacular. He had every slang saying as soon
as it was out, and by this used to triumph over.
his rival Caniche, who never could follow his.
phraseology.

"Hallo, Caniche!" he said; "how are you?
What's up?—running the rig on the boys here!
telling Charley Potts his daubs are first-rate?
Pickles!—We know all that game, don't we,
Charley? What do you want for it, Charley?
—How are you, Mr. Bowie? what's fresh with
you, sir? Too proud to come and have a cut
of mutton with me and Mrs. S. a-Sunday, I
suppose? Some good fellers coming, too; Mug-
ger from the Cracksideum, and Talboys and Sir
Paul Potter—leastways I've asked him.—Well,
Charley, what's the figure for this lot, eh?"

"I'll trouble you not to 'Charley' me, Mr..
Stump, or whatever your infernal name is!" said
Potts, folding his arms and puffing out his smoke.

savagely. "I don't want any Havannah cigars, nor silk handkerchiefs, nor painted canaries, nor any thing else in your line, sir; and I want your confounded patronage least of all!"

"Good boy, Charley! very good boy!" said Stompff, calmly pulling his whisker through his teeth—"shouldn't lose his temper, though. Come and dine a-Sunday, Charley." Mr. Potts said something, which the historian is not bound to repeat, turned on his heel and walked away.

Mr. Stompff was not a bit disconcerted at this treatment. He merely stuck his tongue in his cheek, and looking at the men standing round, said, "He's on the high ropes, is Master Charley! Some of you fellows have been lending him half-a-crown, or that fool Caniche has bought one of his pictures for seven-and-six! Now, has any body any thing new to show, eh?" Of course every body had something new to show to the great Stompff, the enterprising Stompff, the liberal Stompff, whose cheques were as good as notes of the Bank of England. How they watched his progress, and how their hearts beat as he loitered

before their works! Jupp, who had a bed-ridden
wife, a dear pretty little woman recovering from
rheumatic fever at Adalbert Villa, Elgiva Road,
St. John's Wood; Smethurst, who had a 25*l.* bill
coming due in a fortnight, and had three-and-
sevenpence wherewith to meet it; Vogelstadt, who
had been beguiled into leaving Düsseldorf for
London on the rumours of English riches and
English patronage, and whose capital studies of
birds in the snow, and *treibejagds*, and boar-hunts,
had called forth universal laudation, but had not
as yet entrapped a single purchaser, so that Vogelstadt, who had come down not discontentedly to
living on bread-and-milk, had notions of mort-
gaging his ancestral thumb-ring to procure even
those trifling necessaries,—how they all glared
with expectation as the ex-singing-bird-importer
passed their pictures in review! That worthy
took matters very easily, strolling along with his
hands in his pockets, glancing at the easels and
along the walls, occasionally nodding his head in
approval, or shrugging his shoulders in deprecia-
tion, but never saying a word until he stopped

opposite a well-placed figure-subject to which he
devoted a two-minutes' close scrutiny, and then
uttered this frank though *argot*-tinged criticism,
" That'll hit 'em up! that'll open their eyelids, by
Jove! Whose is it?"

The picture represented a modern ballroom, in
a corner of which a man of middle age, his arms
tightly folded across his breast, was intently watching the movements of a young girl, just starting off
in a *valse* with a handsome dashing young partner.
The expressions in the two faces were admirably
defined: in the man's was a deep earnest devotion
not unmingled with passion and with jealousy, his
tightly-clenched mouth, his deep-set earnest eyes,
settled in rapt adoration on the girl, showed the
earnestness of his feeling, so did the rigidly-fixed
arms, and the *pose* of the figure, which, originally
careless, had become hardened and angular through
intensity of feeling. The contrast was well marked:
in the girl's face, which was turned toward the
man while her eyes were fixed on him, was a
bright saucy triumph, brightening her eyes, in-
flating her little nostrils, curving the corners of

her mouth, while her figure was light and airy, just obedient to the first notes of the *valse*, balancing itself as it were on the arm of her partner before starting off down the dance. All the accessories were admirable: the dreary wallflowers ranged round the room, the chaperons nid-nodding together on the rout-seats, paterfamilias despondingly consulting his watch, the wearied hostess, and the somnolently-inclined musicians,—all were there, portrayed not merely by a facile hand but by a man conversant with society. The title of the picture, " Sic vos non vobis," was written on a bit of paper stuck into the frame, on the other corner of which was a card bearing the words " Mr. Geoffrey Ludlow."

" Ah !" said Stompff, who, after carefully scanning the picture close and then from a distance, had read the card—" at last ! Geoffrey Ludlow's going to fulfil the promise which he's been showing this ten years ! A late birth, but a fine babby now it's born ! That's the real thing and no flies ! That's about as near a good thing as I've seen this long time—that; come, you'll say the same! That's a good picture, Mr. Wrigley!"

" Ah!" said old Tom, coming up at the moment, " you've made another lucky hit if you've bought that, Mr. Stompff! Geoff is so confoundedly undecided, so horribly weak in all things, that he's been all this time making up his mind whether he really would paint a good picture or not. But he's decided at last, and he has painted a clipper."

" Ye-es! said Stompff, whose first enthusiasm had by no means died away—on the contrary, he thought so well of the picture that he had within himself determined to purchase it ; but his business caution was coming over him strongly. " Yes! it's a clipper, as you say, Wrigley; but it's a picture which would take all a fellow knew to work it. Throw that into the market—where are you? Pouf! gone! no one thinking of it. Judicious advertisement, judicious squaring of those confounded fellows of the press ; a little dinner at the Albion or the Star and Garter to two or three whom *we* know ; and then the wonderful grasp of modern life, the singular manner in which the

great natural feelings are rendered, the micro-
scopic observation, and the power of detail—"

"Yes, yes," said Tom Wrigley; "for which,
see *Catalogue of Stompff's Gallery of Modern Paint-
ers*, price 6*d*. Spare yourself, you unselfish en-
courager of talent, and spare Geoff's blushes;
for here he is.—Did you hear what Stompff was
saying on, Geoff?"

As he spoke, there came slouching up, shoul-
dering his way through the crowd, a big, heavily-
built man of about forty years of age, standing
over six feet, and striking in appearance, if not
prepossessing. Striking in appearance from his
height, which was even increased by his great
shock head of dark-brown hair standing upright
on his forehead, but curling in tight crisp waves
round the back and poll of his head; from his
great prominent brown eyes, which, firmly set
in their large thickly-carved lids, flashed from
under an overhanging pair of brows; from his
large heavy nose, thick and fleshy, yet with lithe
sensitive nostrils; from his short upper and pro-
truding thick under lip; from the length of his

chin and the massive heaviness of his jaw, though
the heavy beard greatly concealed the formation
of the lower portion of his face. A face which
at once evoked attention, which no one passed
by without noticing, which people at first called
" odd," and " singular," and " queer," according to their vocabulary; then, following the same
rule, pronounced "ugly," or " hideous," or "gro-
tesque"—allowing all the time that there " was
something very curious in it." But a face which,
when seen in animation or excitement, in reflex
of the soul within, whose every thought was
legibly portrayed in its every expression, in
light or shade, with earnest watchful eyes, and
knit brows and quivering nostrils and working
lips; or, on the other hand, with its mouth full
of sound big white teeth gleaming between its
ruddy lips, and its eyes sparkling with pure
merriment or mischief;—then a face to be preferred to all the dolly inanities of the Household
Brigade, or even the matchless toga - draped
dummies in Mr. Truefitt's window. This was
Geoffrey Ludlow, whom every body liked, but

who was esteemed to be so weak and vacillating,
so infirm of purpose, so incapable of succeeding
in his art or in his life, as to have been always
regarded as an object of pity rather than envy;
as a man who was his own worst enemy, and of
whom nothing could be said. He had apparently
caught some words of the conversation, for when
he arrived at the group a smile lit up his homely
features, and his teeth glistened again in the gaslight.

"What are you fellows joking about?" he
asked, while he roared with laughter, as if with
an anticipatory relish of the fun. "Some chaff
at my expense, eh? Something about my not
having made up my mind to do something or
not; the usual nonsense, I suppose?"

"Not at all, Geoff," said Tom Wrigley. "The
question asked by Mr. Stompff here was—whether
you wished to sell this picture, and what you asked
for it."

"Ah!" said Geoffrey Ludlow, his lips closing
and the fun dying out of his eyes. "Well, you see
it's of course a compliment for you, Mr. Stompff, to

ask the question; but I've scarcely made up my mind—whether—and indeed as to the price—"

"Stuff, Geoff! What rubbish you talk!" said Charley Potts, who had rejoined the group. "You know well enough that you painted the picture for sale. You know equally well that the price is two hundred guineas. Are you answered, Mr. Stump?"

Ludlow started forward with a look of annoyance, but Stompff merely grinned, and said quietly, "I take it at the price, and as many more as Mr. Ludlow will paint of the same sort; stock, lock, and barrel, I'll have the whole bilin. Must change the title though, Ludlow, my boy. None of your Sic wos non thingummy; none of your Hebrew classics for the British public. 'The Vow,' or 'The Last Farewell,' or something in that line.—Very neatly done of you, Charley, my boy; very neat bit of dealing, I call it. I ought to deduct four-and-nine from the next fifteen shillin' commission you get; but I'll make it up to you this way,—you've evidently all the qualities of a salesman; come and be my clerk, and

I'll stand thirty shillings a-week and a commission on the catalogues."

Charley Potts was too delighted at his friend's success to feel annoyance at these remarks; he merely shook his fist laughingly, and was passing on, with his arm through Ludlow's; but the vivacious dealer, who had rapidly calculated where he could plant his newly-acquired purchase, and what percentage he could make on it, was not to be thus balked.

"Look here!" said he; "a bargain's a bargain, ain't it? People say your word's as good as your bond, and all that. Pickles! You drop down to my office to-morrow, Ludlow, and there'll be an agreement for you to sign—all straight and reg'lar, you know. And come and cut your mutton with me and Mrs. S. at Velasquez Villa, Nottin' 'Ill, on Sunday, at six. No sayin' no, because I won't hear it. We'll wet our connection in a glass of Sham. And bring Charley with you, if his dress-coat ain't up! You know, Charley! Tar, tar!" And highly delighted with himself, and with the full conviction that he had rendered himself thoroughly delightful to his hearers, the great man waddled off to his brougham.

Meanwhile the news of the purchase had spread through the rooms, and men were hurrying up on all sides to congratulate Ludlow on his success. The fortunate man seemed, however, a little dazed with his triumph; he shook all the outstretched hands cordially, and said a few commonplaces of thanks, intermingled with doubts as to whether he had not been too well treated; but on the first convenient opportunity he slipped away, and sliding a shilling into the palm of Flexor the model, who, being by this time very drunk, had arranged his hair in a curl on his forehead, and was sitting on the bench in the hall after his famous rendering of George the Fourth of blessed memory, Geoff seized his hat and coat and let himself out. The fresh night-air revived him wonderfully, and he was about starting off at his usual headstrong pace, when he heard a low dismal moan, and looking round, he saw a female figure cowering in a doorway. The next instant he was kneeling by her side.

CHAPTER III.

THE strange caprices of Fashion were never more
strangely illustrated than by her fixing upon
St. Barnabas Square as one of her favourite
localities. There are men yet living among us
whose mothers had been robbed on their way
from Ranelagh in crossing the spot, then a dreary
swampy marsh, on which now stands the city of
palaces known as Cubittopolis. For years on
years it remained in its dismal condition, until
an enterprising builder, seeing the army of civi-
lisation advancing with grand strides south-west-
ward, and perceiving at a glance the immediate
realisation ' of an enormous profit on his outlay,
bought up the entire estate, had it thoroughly
cleansed and drained, and proceeded to erect
thereon a series of terraces, places, and squares,

each vying with the other in size, perfection of finish, and, let it be said, general ghastliness. The houses in St. Barnabas Square resemble those in Chasuble Crescent, and scarcely differ in any particular from the eligible residences in Reredos Road : they are all very tall, and rather thin ; they have all enormous porticoes, over which are little conservatories, railed in with ecclesiastical ironwork; dismal little back - rooms no bigger than warm-baths, but described as " libraries" by the house - agents ; gaunt drawing - rooms connected by an arch; vast landings, leading on to other little conservatories, where " blacks," old flower-pots, and a few geranium stumps, are principally conserved; and a series of gaunt towny bedrooms. In front they have Mr. Swiveller's prospect, — a delightful view of over-the-way ; across the bit of square enclosure like a green pocket-handkerchief; while at the back they look immediately on to the back - premises of other eligible residences. The enterprising builder has done his best for his neighbourhood, but he has been unable to neutralise the effects of the neigh-

bouring Thames; and the consequence is, that
during the winter months a chronic fog drifts
up from the pleasant Kentish marshes, and finding ample room and verge enough, settles per-
manently down in the St. Barnabas district;
while in the summer, the new roads which in-
tersect the locality, being mostly composed of a
chalky foundation, peel off under every passing
wheel, and emit enormous clouds of dust, which
are generally drifting on the summer wind into
the eyes and mouths of stray passengers, and in
at the doors and windows of regular residents.
Yet this is one of Fashion's chosen spots: here
in this stronghold of stucco reside scores of those
whose names and doings the courtly journalist
delighteth to chronicle; hither do county magnates bring, to furnished houses, their wives and
daughters, leaving them to entertain those of the
proper set during the three summer months, while
they, the county magnates themselves, are sleeping the sleep of the just on the benches of the
House of Commons, or nobly discharging their
duty to their country by smoking cigars on the

terrace; here reside men high up in the great West-end public offices, commissioners and secretaries, anxious to imbue themselves with the scent of the rose, and *vivre près d'elle*, City magnates, judges of the land, and counsel learned in the law. The situation is near to Westminster for the lawyers and politicians; and the address has quite enough of the true ring about it to make it much sought after by all those who go-in for a fashionable neighbourhood.

A few hours before the events described in the preceding chapters took place, a brougham, perfectly appointed, and drawn by a splendid horse, came dashing through the fog and driving mist, and pulled up before one of the largest houses in St. Barnabas Square. The footman jumped from the box, and was running to the door, when, in obedience to a sharp voice, he stopped, and the occupant of the vehicle, who had descended, crossed the pavement with rapid strides, and opened the door with a pass-key. He strode quickly through the hall, up the staircase, and into the drawing-room, round which he took a rapid glance. The room was empty; the gas was lit, and a fire burned brightly on the hearth; while an open piano, covered with music, on the one side of the fire-place, and a book turned down with open leaves, showed that the occupants had but recently left. The new-comer, finding himself alone, walked to the mantelpiece, and leaning his back against it, passed his hands rapidly across his forehead; then plunging both of them into his pockets, seemed lost in thought. The gaslight showed him to be a man of about sixty years of age, tall, wiry, well-proportioned; his head was bald, with a fringe of grayish hair, his forehead broad, his eyes deep-set, his mouth thin-lipped and ascetic; he wore two little strips of whisker, but his chin was closely shaved. He was dressed in high stiff shirt-collars, a blue-silk neckerchief with white dots, in which gleamed a carbuncle pin; a gray overcoat, under which was a cutaway riding-coat, high waistcoat with onyx buttons, and tight-fitting cord-trousers. This was George Brakespere, third Earl Beauport, of whom and of whose family it behoves one to speak in detail.

They were *novi homines*, the Brakespcres, though they always claimed to be sprung from ancient Norman blood. Only seventy years ago old Martin Brakespcre was a woolstapler in Uttoxeter; and though highly respected for the wealth he was reported to have amassed, was very much jeered at privately, and with bated breath, for keeping an apocryphal genealogical tree hanging up in his back-shop, and for invariably boasting, after his second glass of grog at the Greyhound, about his lineage. But when, after old Martin had been some score years quietly resting in Uttoxeter churchyard, his son Sir Richard Brakespere, who had been successively solicitor and attorney general, was raised to the peerage, and took his seat on the woolsack as Baron Beauport, Lord High Chancellor of England, the Herald's College, and all the rest of the genealogical authorities, said that the line was thoroughly made out, and received the revival of the ancient title with the greatest laudation. A wiry, fox-headed, thin chip of a lawyer, the first Baron Beauport, as knowing as a ferret, and not unlike one in the face. He administered the laws of his country very well, and he lent some of the money he had inherited from his father to the sovereign of his country and the first gentleman in Europe at a very high rate of interest, it is said. Rumour reports that he did not get all his money back again, taking instead thereof an increase in rank, and dying, at an advanced age, as Earl Beauport, succeeded in his title and estates by his only son, Theodore Brakespere, by courtesy Viscount Caterham.

When his father died, Lord Caterham, the second Earl Beauport, was nearly fifty years old, a prim little gentleman who loved music and wore a wig; a dried-up chip of a little man, who lived in a little house in Hans Place with an old servant, a big violoncello, and a special and peculiar breed of pug-dogs. To walk out with the pug-dogs in the morning, to be carefully dressed and tittivated and buckled and curled by the old servant in the afternoon, and either to play the violoncello in a Beethoven or Mozart selection with some other old amateur fogies, or to be present at a performance of chamber-music, or phil-

harmonics, or oratorio-rehearsals in the evening,
constituted the sole pleasure of the second Earl
Beauport's life. He never married; and at his
death, some fifteen years after his father's, the
title and, with the exception of a few legacies to
musical charities, the estates passed to his cousin
George Brakespere, Fellow of Lincoln College,
Oxon, and then of Little Milman Street, Bed-
ford Row, and the Northern Circuit, briefless
barrister.

Just in the very nick of time came the peerage
and the estates to George Brakespere, for he was
surrounded by duns, and over head and ears in
love. With all his hard work at Oxford, and he
had·worked hard, he had the reputation of being
the best bowler at Bullingdon, and the hardest
rider after hounds; of having the best old port
and the finest cigars (it was before the days of
claret and short pipes), and the best old oak furniture, library of books, and before-letter proofs
in the University. All these could not be paid
for out of an undergraduate's income; and the
large remainder of unpaid bills hung round him

and plagued him heavily long after he had left
Oxford and been called to the bar. It was horribly
up-hill work getting a connection among the at-
torneys; he tried writing for reviews, and succeeded, but earned very little money. And then,
on circuit, at an assize-ball, he fell in love with
Gertrude Carrington, a haughty county beauty,
only daughter of Sir Joshua Carrington, Chair-
man of Quarter Sessions; and that nearly finished
him. Gertrude Carrington was very haughty and
very wilful; she admired the clever face and the
bold bearing of the young barrister; but in all
probability she would have thought no more of
him, had not the eminent Sir Joshua, who kept
his eyes very sharply about him, marked the
flirtation, and immediately expressed his total dis-
approval of it. That was enough for Gertrude,
and she at once went in for George Brakespere,
heart and soul. She made no objection to a clan-
destine correspondence, and responded regularly
and warmly to George's passionate letters. She
gave him two or three secret meetings under an
old oak in a secluded part of her father's park,—

Homershams was a five-hours' journey from town,
—and these assignations always involved George's
sleeping at an inn, and put him to large expense;
and when she came up to stay with her cousins
in town, she let him know all the parties to which
they were going, and rendered him a mendicant
for invitations. When the change of fortune
came, and George succeeded to the title, Sir
Joshua succumbed at once, and became anxious
for the match. Had George inherited money
only, it is probable that from sheer wilfulness
Gertrude would have thrown him over; but the
notion of being a countess, of taking precedence
and *pas* of all the neighbouring gentry, had its
influence, and they were married. Two sons were
born to them,—Viscount Caterham and the Hon.
Lionel Brakespere,—and a daughter, who only
survived her birth a few weeks. As Earl Beauport, George Brakespere retained the energy and
activity of mind and body, the love of exercise
and field-sports, the clear brain and singleness of
purpose, which had distinguished him as a com-
moner: but there was a skeleton in his house,

whose bony fingers touched his heart in his gayest moments, numbed his energies, and warped his usefulness; whose dread presence he could not escape from, whose chilling influence nor wine, nor work, nor medicine, nor gaiety, could palliate. It was ever present in a tangible shape; he knew his weakness and wickedness in permitting it to conquer him,—he strove against it, but vainly; and in the dead watches of the night often he lay broad awake railing against the fate which had mingled so bitter an ingredient in his cup of happiness.

The door swung open and the Countess entered, a woman nearly fifty now, but not looking her age by at least eight years. A tall handsome woman, with the charms of her former beauty mellowed but not impaired: the face was more full, but the firm chiselling of the nose and lips, the brightness of the eyes, the luxurious dark gloss of the hair were there still. As she entered her husband advanced to meet her; and as he touched her forehead with his lips, she laid her hand on his, and asked, " What news ?"

He shook his head sadly, and said, "The worst."

"The worst!" she repeated, faintly; "he's not dead? Beauport, you—you would not say it in that way—he's not dead?"

"I wish to God he were!" said Lord Beauport through his teeth. "I wish it had pleased God to take him years and years ago! No; he's not dead." Then throwing himself into a chair,. and staring vacantly at the fire, he repeated, "I wish to God he were!"

"Any thing but that!" said the Countess, with a sense of immense relief; "any thing but that! whatever he has done may be atoned for, and repented, and—But what has he done? where is he? have you seen Mr. Farquhar?"

"I have—and I know all. Gertrude, Lionel is a scoundrel and a criminal—no, don't interrupt me!—I myself have prosecuted and transported men for less crimes than he has committed; years ago he would have been hanged. He is a forger!"

"A forger!"

"He has forged the names of two of his friends—old brother officers; Lord Hinchenbrook is one, and young Latham the other—to bills for five thousand pounds. I've had the bills in my hands, and seen letters from the men denying their signatures to-night, and—"

"But Lionel—where is he? in prison?"

"No; he saw the crash coming, and fled from it. Farquhar showed me a blotted letter from him, written from Liverpool, saying in a few lines that he had disgraced us all, that he was on the point of sailing under a feigned name for Australia, and that we should never see him again."

"Never see him again! my boy, my own darling boy!" and Lady Beauport burst into an agony of tears.

"Gertrude," said her husband, when the first wild storm of grief had subsided, "calm yourself for one instant."

He rang the bell, and to the servant answering it, said:

"Tell Lord Caterham I wish to speak to him,

and beg Miss Maurice to be good enough to step here."

Lady Beauport was about to speak, but the Earl said coldly:

" I wish it, if you please ;" and reiterated his commands to the servant, who left the room. " I have fully decided, Gertrude, on the step I am about to take. To-morrow those forged bills will be mine. I saw young Latham at Farquhar's, and he said—" Lord Beauport's voice shook here —" said every thing that was kind and noble; and Hinchenbrook has said the same to Farquhar. It—it cannot be kept quiet, of course. Every club is probably ringing with it now ; but they will let me have the bills. And from this moment, Gertrude, that boy's name must never be uttered, save in our prayers—in our prayers for his forgiveness and—and repentance—by you, his mother ; by me his father,—nor by any one in this house. He is dead to us for ever !"

" Beauport, for Heaven's sake—"

" I swear it, Gertrude, I swear it ! and most solemnly will keep the oath. I have sent for

Caterham, who must know, of course; his good sense will approve what I have done; and for Annie, she is part of our household now, and must be told. Dead to us all henceforth; dead to us all!"

He sank into a chair opposite the fire and buried his face in his hands, but roused himself at advancing footsteps. The door opened, and a servant entered, pushing before him a library-chair fitted on large wheels, in which sat a man of about thirty, of slight spare frame, with long arms and thin womanly hands — a delicately-handsome man, with a small head, soft gray eyes, and an almost feminine mouth; a man whom Nature had intended for an Apollo, whom fortune had marked for her sport, blighting his childhood with some mysterious disease for which the doctors could find neither name nor cure, sapping his marrow and causing his legs to wither into the shrunken and useless members which now hung loosely before him utterly without strength, almost without shape, incapable of bearing his weight, and rendering him maimed,

crippled, blasted for life. This was Viscount
Caterham, Earl Beauport's eldest son, and heir
to his title and estates. His father cast one
short, rapid glance at him as he entered, and
then turned to the person who immediately
followed him.

This was a tall girl of two-and-twenty, of
rounded form and winning expression. Her features were by no means regular; her eyes were
brown and sleepy; she had a pert inquisitive
nose; and when she smiled, in her decidedly
large mouth gleamed two rows of strong white
teeth. Her dark - brown hair was simply and
precisely arranged; for she had but a humble
opinion of her own charms, and objected to any
appearance of coquetry. She was dressed in a
tight-fitting black silk, with linen collar and
cuffs, and her hands and feet were small and
perfectly shaped. Darling Annie Maurice, orphan
daughter of a second cousin of my lord's, trans-
planted from a suburban curacy to be companion
and humble friend of my lady, the one bright bit
of sunshine and reality in that palace of ghastly

stucco and sham. Even now as she came in
Lord Beauport seemed to feel the cheering influence of her presence, and his brow relaxed for
an instant as he stepped forward and offered his
hand; after taking which she, with a bow to the
Countess, glided round and stood by Lord Caterham's chair.

Lord Caterham was the first to speak.

"You sent for us—for Annie and me, sir,"
he said in a low tremulous voice; "I trust you
have no bad news of Lionel."

Lady Beauport hid her face in her hands;
but the Earl, who had resumed his position against
the mantelpiece, spoke firmly.

"I sent for you, Caterham, and for you, Annie,
as members of my family, to tell you that Lionel
Brakespere's name must never more be mentioned
in this house. He has disgraced himself, and us
through him; and though we cannot wipe away
that disgrace, we must strive as far as possible to
blot him out from our memories and our lives.
You know, both of you,—at least you, Caterham,
know well enough,—what he has been to me—

the love I had for him—the—yes, my God, the
pride I had in him!"

His voice broke here, and he passed his hand
across his eyes. In the momentary pause Annie
Maurice glanced up at Lord Caterham, and marked
his face distorted as with pain, and his head re-
clining on his chest. Then, gulping down the
knot rising in his throat, the Earl continued:

"All that is over now; he has left the country,
and the chances are that we shall never see nor
even hear from him again." A moan from the
Countess shook his voice for a second, but he proceeded: "It was to tell you this that I sent for
you. You and I, Caterham, will have to enter
upon this subject once more to-morrow, when
some business arrangements have to be made. On
all other occasions, recollect, it is tabooed. Let his
name be blotted out from our memories, and let
him be as if he had never lived."

As Earl Beauport ceased speaking he gathered
himself together and walked towards the door,
never trusting himself to look for an instant towards where his wife sat cowering in grief, lest

his firmness should desert him. Down the stairs he went, until entering his library he shut the door behind him, locked it, and throwing himself into his chair, leant his head on the desk, and covering it with his hands gave way to a passion of sobs which shook his strong frame as though he were convulsed. Then rising, he went to the book-case, and taking out a large volume, opened it, and turned to the page immediately succeeding the cover. It was a big old-fashioned Bible, bound in calf, with a hideous ancient woodcut as a frontispiece, representing the Adoration of the Wise Men; but the page to which Lord Beauport turned, yellow with age, was inscribed in various-coloured inks, many dim and faded, with the names of the old Brakespere family, and the dates of their births, marriages, and deaths. Old Martin Brakespere's headed the list; then came his son's, with " created Baron Beauport" in the lawyer's own skimpy little hand, in which also was entered the name of the musical-amateur peer, his son; then came George Brakespere's bold entry of his own name and his wife's, and of the names of their two sons. Over the last entry Lord Beauport paused for a few minutes, glaring at it with eyes which did not see it, but which had before them a chubby child, a bright handsome Eton boy, a dashing guardsman, a " swell" loved and petted by all, a fugitive skulking in an assumed name in the cabin of a sea-tossed ship; then he took up a pen and ran it through the entry backwards and forwards until the name was completely blotted out; and then he fell again into his train of thought. The family dinner-hour was long since past; the table was laid, all was ready, and the French cook and the grave butler were in despair; but Lord Beauport still sat alone in his library with old Martin Brakespere's Bible open before him.

CHAPTER IV.

It is cheap philosophy to moralise on the importance of events led up to by the merest trifles; but the subject comes so frequently before us as to furnish innumerable pegs whereon the week-day preacher may hang up his little garland of reflections, his little wreath of homely truisms. If Ned Waldron had not been crossing into the Park at the exact moment when the shortsighted Godalming banker was knocked down by the hansom at the Corner, he would have still been enjoying eighty pounds a-year as a temporary extra-clerk at Whitehall instead of groaning over the villanous extortion of the malt-tax, as a landed proprietor of some thousands of inherited acres. If Dr. Weston's red-lamp over the surgery-door had been blown out when the servant rushed off for medical advice

for Master Percy Buckmaster's earache, the eminent apothecary would nevér have had the chance
of which he so skilfully availed himself—of paying
dutiful attention to Mrs. Buckmaster, and finally
stepping into the shoes of her late husband, the
wealthy Indian indigo-planter.

If Geoffrey Ludlow, dashing impetuously onward in his career, had not heard that long low
heart-breaking moan, he might have gone on
leading his easy, shiftless, drifting life, with no
break greater than the excitement consequent on
the sale of a picture or the accomplishment of a
resolution. But he *did* hear it, and, rare thing in
him, acting at once on his first impulse, he dropped
on his knees just in time to catch the fainting form
in his outstretched arms. That same instant he
would have shrunk back if he could; but it was
too late; that same instant there came across him
a horrible feeling of the ludicrousness of his position: there at midnight in a London thoroughfare
holding in his arms—what? a drunken tramp,
perhaps; a vagrant well known to the Mendicity
Society; a gin-soddened street-walker, who might

requite his good Samaritanism with a leer and a
laugh, or an oath and a blow. And yet the groan
seemed to come from the lowest depths of a wrung
and suffering heart; and the appearance—no, there
could be no mistake about that. That thin, almost
emaciated, figure; those pinched features; drawn,
haggard, colourless cheeks; that brow, half hidden
by the thick, damp, matted hair, yet in its deep
lines and indentations revealing the bitter work-
ings of the mind; the small thin bony hands now
hanging flaccid and motionless—all these, if there
were any thing real in this life, were outward
semblances such as mere imposters could not have
brought forward in the way of trade.

Not one of them was lost on Geoffrey Ludlow,
who, leaning over the prostrate figure, narrowly
scanned its every feature, bent his face towards
the mouth, placed his hands on the heart, and
then, thoroughly alarmed, looked round and called
for aid. Perhaps his excitement had something to
do with it, but Geoff's voice fell flat and limp on
the thick damp air, and there was no response,
though he shouted again and again. But pre-

sently the door whence he had issued opened
widely, and in the midst of a gush of tobacco-
smoke a man came out, humming a song, twirling
a stick, and striding down the street. Again
Geoffrey Ludlow shouted, and this time with success, for the new-comer stopped suddenly, took
his pipe from his mouth, and turning his head
towards the spot whence the voice proceeded, he
called out, simply but earnestly, "Hallo there!
what's the row?"

Ludlow recognised the speaker at once. It
was Charley Potts, and Geoffrey hailed him by
name.

"All right!" said Charley in return. "You've
picked up my name fast enough, my pippin; but
that don't go far. Better known than trusted is
your obedient servant, C. P. Hallo, Geoff, old
man, is it you? Why, what the deuce have you
got there? an 'omeless poor, that won't move
on, or a —— By George, Geoff, this is a bad
case!" He had leant over the girl's prostrate
body, and had rapidly felt her pulse and listened
at her heart. "This woman's dying of inanition

and prostration. I know it, for I was in the red-bottle and Plaster-of-Paris-horse line before I went in for Art. She must be looked to at once, or she'll slip off the hooks while we're standing by her. You hold on here, old man, while I run back and fetch the brandy out of Dabb's room; I know where he keeps it. Chafe her hands, will you, Geoff? I sha'n't be a second."

Charley Potts rushed off, and left Geoffrey still kneeling by the girl's side. In obedience to his friend's instructions, he began mechanically to chafe her thin worn hands; but as he rubbed his own over them to and fro, to and fro, he peered into her face, and wondered dreamily what kind of eyes were hidden behind the dropped lids, and what was the colour of the hair hanging in dank thick masses over the pallid brow. Even now there began to spring in his mind a feeling of wonder not unmixed with alarm, as to what would be thought of him, were he discovered in his then position; whether his motives would be rightly construed; whether he were not acting somewhat indiscreetly in so far committing himself: for Geoffrey Ludlow had been brought up in the strict school of dire respectability, where a lively terror of rendering yourself liable to Mrs. Grundy's remarks is amongst the doctrines most religiously inculcated. But a glance at the form before him gave him fresh assurance; and when Charley Potts returned he found his friend rubbing away with all his energy.

"Here it is," said Charley; "Dabb's particular. I know it's first-rate, for Dabb only keeps it medicinally, taking Sir Felix Booth Bart. as his ordinary tipple. I know this water-of-life-of-cognac of old, sir, and always have internal qualms of conscience when I go to see Dabb, which will not be allayed until I have had what Caniche calls a suspicion. Hold her head for a second, Geoff, while I put the flask to her mouth. There! Once more, Geoff. Ah! I thought so. Her pulse is moving now, old fellow, and she'll rouse in a bit; but it was very nearly a case of Walker."

"Look at her eyes—they're unclosing."

" Not much wonder in that, is there, my boy? though it is odd, perhaps. A glass of brandy has made many people shut their eyes before now; but as to opening them—Hallo! steady there!"

He said this as the girl, her eyes glaring straight before her, attempted to raise herself into an erect position, but after a faint struggle dropped back, exclaiming feebly :

" I cannot, I cannot."

" Of course you can't, my dear," said Charley Potts, not unkindly; " of course you can't. You mustn't think of attempting it either. I say, Geoff,"—(this was said in a lower tone)—"look out for the policeman when he comes round, and give him a hail. Our young friend here must be looked after at once, and he'd better take her in a cab to the workhouse."

As he said the last words, Geoffrey Ludlow felt the girl's hand which he held thrill between his, and, bending down, thought he saw her lips move.

" What's the matter?" said Charley Potts.

" It's very strange," replied Geoffrey; " I could swear I heard her say ' Not there!' and yet—"

" Likely enough been there before, and knows the treatment. However, we must get her off at once, or she'll go to grief; so let us—"

" Look here, Charley : I don't like the notion of this woman's going to a workhouse, specially as she seems to—object, eh ? Couldn't we—isn't there any one where we could—where she could lodge for a night or two, until—the doctor, you know—one might see ? Confound it all, Charley, you know I never can explain exactly ; can't you help me, eh ?"

" What a stammering old idiot it is !" said Charley Potts, laughing. " Yes, I see what you mean — there's Flexor's wife lives close by, in Little Flotsam Street — keeps a lodging-house. If she's not full, this young party can go in there. She's all right now so far as stopping it is concerned, but she'll want a deal of looking after yet. O, by Jove ! I left Rollit in at the Titians, the army-doctor, you know, who sketches so well. Let's get her into Flexor's, and I'll fetch Rollit to look at her. Easy now ! Up !"

They raised her to her feet, and half-supported, half-carried her round the church and across the broad road, and down a little bystreet on the other side. There Charley Potts stopped at a door, and knocking at it, was soon confronted by a buxom middle-aged woman, who started with surprise at seeing the group.

" Lor, Mr. Potts! what can have brought you 'ere, sir? Flexor's not come in, sir, yet—at them nasty Titiums, he is, and joy go with him. If you're wanting him, sir, you'd better—"

" No, Mrs. Flexor, we don't want your husband just now. Here's Mr. Ludlow, who—"

" Lord, and so it is! but seeing nothing but the nape of your neck, sir, I did not recognise—"

" All right, Mrs. Flexor," said Geoffrey ; " we want to know if your house is full. If not, here is a poor woman for whom we—at least Mr. Potts —and I myself, for the matter of that—"

" Stuttering again, Geoff! What stuff! Here, Mrs. Flexor, we want a room for this young woman to sleep in ; and just help us in with her at once into your parlour, will you? and let us put her down there while I run round for the doctor."

It is probable that Mrs. Flexor might have raised objections to this proposition; but Charley Potts was a favourite with her, and Geoffrey Ludlow was a certain source of income to her husband ; so she stepped back while the men caught up their burden, who all this time had been resting, half-fainting, on Geoffrey's shoulder, and carried her into the parlour. Here they placed her in a big, frayed, ragged easy-chair, with all its cushion-stuffing gone, and palpable bits of shaggy wool peering through its arms and back; and after dragging this in front of the expiring fire, and bidding Mrs. Flexor at once prepare some hot gruel, Charley Potts rushed away to catch Dr. Rollit.

And now Geoffrey Ludlow, left to himself once more (for the girl was lying back in the chair, still with unclosing eyes, and had apparently relapsed into a state of stupor), began to turn the events of the past hour in his mind, and to wonder very much at the position in which he found himself. Here he was in a room in a house which he had never before entered, shut up with a

girl of whose name or condition he was as yet
entirely ignorant, of whose very existence he had
only just known ; he, who had always shirked any
thing which afforded the smallest chance of adventure, was actually taking part in a romance. And
yet — nonsense! here was a starving wanderer,
whom he and his friend had rescued from the
street; an ordinary every-day case, familiar in a
thousand phases to the relieving-officers and the
poor-law guardians, who, after her certain allow-
ance of warmth, and food, and physic, would start
off to go—no matter where, and do—no matter
what. And yet he certainly had not been deceived
in thinking of her faint protest when Charley
proposed to send her to the workhouse. She had
spoken then; and though the words were so few
and the tone so low, there was something in the
latter which suggested education and refinement.
Her hands too, her poor thin hands, were long
and well-shaped, with tapering fingers and filbert-
nails, and bore no traces of hard work : and her face
—ah, he should be better able to see her face now !

He turned, and taking the flaring candle from

the table, held it above her head. Her eyes were
still closed; but as he moved, they opened wide,
and fixed themselves on him. Such large, deep-
violet eyes, with long sweeping lashes! such a long,
solemn, steadfast gaze, in which his own eyes were
caught fast, and remained motionless. Then on to
his hand, leaning on the arm of the chair, came
the cold clammy pressure of feeble fingers; and in
his ear, bent and listening, as he saw a fluttering
motion of her lips, murmured very feebly the
words, "Bless you!—saved me!" twice repeated.
As her breath fanned his cheek, Geoffrey Ludlow's
heart beat fast and audibly, his hand shook beneath the light touch of the lithe fingers; but the
next instant the eyelids dropped, the touch relaxed, and a tremulousness seized on the ashy lips.
Geoffrey glanced at her for an instant, and was
rushing in alarm to the door, when it opened, and
Charley Potts entered, followed by a tall grave
man, in a long black beard, whom Potts introduced as Dr. Rollit.

"You're just in time," said Geoffrey; "I was
just going to call for help. She—"

" Pardon me, please," said the doctor, calmly pushing him on one side. " Permit me to—ah!" he continued, after a glance—" I must trouble you to leave the room, Potts, please, and take your friend with you. And just send the woman of the house to me, will you? There is a woman, I suppose?"

" O yes, there is a woman, of course.—Here, Mrs. Flexor, just step up, will you?—Now, Geoff, what are you staring at, man? Do you think the doctor's going to eat the girl? Come on, old fellow; we'll sit on the kitchen-stairs, and catch blackbeetles to pass the time. Come on!"

Geoff roused himself at his friend's touch, and went with him, but in a dreamy sullen manner. When they got into the passage, he remained with outstretched ear, listening eagerly; and when Charley spoke, he savagely bade him hold his tongue. Mr. Potts was so utterly astonished at this conduct, that he continued staring and motionless, and merely gave vent to his feelings in one short low whistle. When the door was opened, Geoffrey Ludlow strode down the passage at once, and confronting the doctor, asked him what news. Dr. Rollit looked his questioner steadily in the eyes for a moment; and when he spoke his tone was softer, his manner less abrupt than before. " There is no special danger, Mr. Ludlow," said he ; " though the girl has had a narrow escape. She has been fighting with cold and want of proper nourishment for days, so far as I can tell."

" Did she say so ?"

" She said nothing ; she has not spoken a word." Dr. Rollit did not fail to notice that here Geoffrey Ludlow gave a sigh of relief. " I but judge from her appearance and symptoms. I have told this good person what to do ; and I will look round early in the morning. I live close by. Now, good-night."

" You are sure as to the absence of danger ?"

" Certain."

" Good - night ; a thousand thanks ! — Mrs. Flexor, mind that your patient has every thing wanted, and that I settle with you.—Now, Charley, come ; what are you waiting for ?"

" Eh ?" said Charley. " Well, I thought that,

after this little excitement, perhaps a glass out of that black bottle which I know Mrs. Flexor keeps on the second shelf in the right-hand cupboard—"

"Get along with you, Mr. Potts!" said Mrs. Flexor, grinning.

"You know you do, Mrs. F.—a glass of that might cheer and not inebriate.—What do you say, Geoff?"

"I say no! You've had quite enough; and all Mrs. Flexor's attention is required elsewhere.—Good-night, Mrs. Flexor; and"—by this time they were in the street—"good-night, Charley."

Mr. Potts, engaged in extracting a short-pipe from the breast-pocket of his pea-jacket, looked up with an abstracted air, and said, "I beg your pardon."

"Good-night, Charley."

"Oh, certainly, if you wish it. Good-night, Geoffrey Ludlow, Esquire; and permit me to add, Hey no nonny! Not a very lucid remark, perhaps, but one which exactly illustrates my state of mind." And Charley Potts filled his pipe, lit it, and remained leaning against the wall, and smoking with much deliberation until his friend was out of sight.

Geoffrey Ludlow strode down the street, the pavement ringing under his firm tread, his head erect, his step elastic, his whole bearing sensibly different even to himself. As he swung along he tried to examine himself as to what was the cause of his sudden light-heartedness; and at first he ascribed it to the sale of his picture, and to the warm promises of support he had received at the hands of Mr. Stompff. But these, though a few hours since they had really afforded him the greatest delight, now paled before the transient glance of two deep-violet eyes, and the scarcely-heard murmur of a feeble voice. " ' Bless you!— saved me!' that's what she said!" exclaimed Geoff, halting for a second and reflecting. " And then the touch of her hand, and the—ah! Charley was right! Hey no nonny is the only language for such an ass as I'm making of myself." So home through the quiet streets, and into his studio, thinking he would smoke one quiet pipe before turning in. There, restlessness, inability to settle

to any thing, mad desire to sketch a certain face
with large eyes, a certain fragile helpless figure,
now prostrate, now half-reclining on a bit of
manly shoulder; a carrying-out of this desire with
a bit of crayon on the studio-wall, several attempts,
constant failure, and consequent disgust. A feeling that ought to have been pleasure, and yet had
a strong tinge of pain at his heart, and a constant
ringing of one phrase, "Bless you!—saved me!"
in his ears. So to bed; where he dreamt he saw
his name, Geoffrey Ludlow, in big black letters at
the bottom of a gold frame, the picture in which
was Keat's "Lamia;" and lo! the Lamia had the
deep-violet eyes of the wanderer in the streets.

CHAPTER V.

THE houses in St. Barnabas Square have an advantage over most other London residences in the possession of a "third room" on the ground-floor. Most people who, purposing to change their domicile, have gone in for a study of the *Times* Supplement or the mendacious catalogues of house-agents, have read of the "noble dining-room, snug breakfast-room, and library," and have found the said breakfast-room to be about the size and depth of a warm-bath, and the "library" a soul-depressing hole just beyond the glazed top of the kitchen-stairs, to which are eventually relegated your old boots, the bust of the friend with whom since he presented it you have had a deadly quarrel, some odd numbers of magazines, and the frame-work of a shower-bath which, in a moment of madness, you bought at a sale and never have been able to fit together.

But the houses in St. Barnabas Square have each, built over what in other neighbourhoods is called "leads,"—a ghastly space where the cats creep stealthily about in the day-time, and whence at night they yowl with preternatural pertinacity,—a fine large room, devoted in most instances to the purposes of billiards, but at Lord Beauport's given up entirely to Lord Caterham. It had been selected originally from its situation on the ground-floor giving the poor crippled lad easy means of exit and entrance, and preventing any necessity for his being carried—for walking was utterly impossible to him—up and down stairs. It was *his* room; and there, and there alone, he was absolute master; there he was allowed to carry out what his mother spoke of as his "fads," what his father called "poor Caterham's odd ways." His brother, Lionel Brakespere, had been in the habit of dropping in there twice or three times a-week, smoking his cigar, turning over the "rum things" on the table, asking ad-

vice which he never took, and lounging round
the room, reading the backs of the books which
he did not understand, and criticising the pictures which he knew nothing about.   It would
have been impossible to tell to what manner of
man the room belonged from a cursory survey
of its contents.   Three fourths of the walls were
covered with large bookcases filled with a hetero-
geneous assemblage of books.   Here a row of
poets, a big quarto *Shakespeare* in six volumes,
followed by *Youatt on the Horse*, *Philip Van
Artevelde*, and Stanhope's *Christian Martyr*.   In
the next shelf Voltaire, all the Tennysons, *Mr.
Sponge's Sporting-Tour*, a work on Farriery, and
Blunt on the Pentateuch.   So the *mélange* ran
throughout the bookshelves; and on the fourth
wall, where hung the pictures, it was not much
better.   For in the centre were Landseer's
" Midsummer-Night's Dream," where that lovely
Titania, unfairy-like if you please, but one of the
most glorious specimens of pictured womanhood,
pillows her fair face under the shadow of that
magnificent ass's-head; and Frith's " Coming of

Age," and Delaroche's "Execution of Lady Jane Grey," and three or four splendid proof-engravings of untouchable Sir Joshua; and among them, dotted here and there, hunting-sketches by Alken, and coaching bits from Fores. Scattered about on tables were pieces of lava from Vesuvius, photographs from Pompeii, a collection of weeds and grasses from the Arctic regions (all duly labelled in the most precise handwriting), a horse's shoe specially adapted for ice-travelling, specimens of egg-shell china, a box of gleaming carpenter's tools, boxes of Tunbridge ware, furs of Indian manufacture, caricature statuettes by Danton, a case of shells, and another of geological specimens. Here stood an easel bearing a half-finished picture, in one corner was a sheaf of walking-sticks, against the wall a rack of whips. Before the fire was a carved-oak writing-desk, and on it, beside the ordinary blotting and writing materials, were an aneroid barometer, a small skeleton clock, and a silver handbell. And at it sat Viscount Caterham, his head drooping, his face pale, his hands idly clasped before him.

Not an unusual position this with him, not unusual by any means when he was alone. In such society as he forced himself to keep—for with him it was more than effort to determine occasionally to shake off his love of solitude, to be present amongst his father's guests, and to receive some few special favourites in his own rooms— he was more than pleasant, he was brilliant and amusing. Big, heavy, good-natured guardsmen, who had contributed nothing to the "go" of the evening, and had nearly tugged off their tawny beards in the vain endeavour to extract something to say, would go away, and growl in deep bass voices over their cigars about "that strordinary f'ler Caterham. Knows a lot, you know, that f'ler, 'bout all sorts things. Can't 'ccive where picks it all up; and as jolly as old boots, by Jove!"

Old friends of Lord Beauport's, now gradually dropping into fogiedom, and clutching year by year more tightly the conventional prejudices instilled into them in early life, listened with elevated eyebrows and dropping jaws to Lord Caterham's outspoken opinions, now clothed in brilliant tropes, now crackling with smart antithesis, but always fresh, earnest, liberal, and vigorous; and when they talked him over in club-windows, these old boys would say that "there was something in that deformed fellow of Beauport's, but that he was all wrong; his mind as warped as his body, by George!" And women,—ah, that was the worst of all,—women would sit and listen to him on such rare occasions as he spoke before them, sit many of them steadfast-eyed and ear-attentive, and would give him smiles and encouraging glances, and then would float away and talk to their next dancing-partner of the strange little man who had such odd ideas, and spoke so—so unlike most people, you know.

He knew it all, this fragile, colourless, delicate cripple, bound for life to his wheel-chair, dependent for mere motion on the assistance of others; a something apart and almost without parallel, helpless as a little child, and yet with the brain, the heart, the passions of a man. No keener observer of outward show, no clearer reader of character than he. From out his deep-set melan-

choly eyes he saw the stare of astonishment,
sometimes the look of disgust, which usually
marked a first introduction to him; his quick ear
caught the would-be compassionate inflection of
the voice addressing him on the simplest matters;
he knew what the old fogies were thinking of, as
they shifted uneasily in their chairs as he spoke;
and he interpreted clearly enough the straying
glances and occasional interjections of the women.
He knew it all, and bore it—bore it as the cross
is rarely borne.

Only three times in his life had there gone up
from his lips a wail to the Father of mercies, a
passionate outpouring of his heart, a wild inquiry
as to why such affliction had been cast upon him.
But three times, and the first of these was when
he was a lad of eighteen. Lord Beauport had
been educated at Charterhouse, where, as every
one knows, Founder's Day is kept with annual
rejoicings. To one of these celebrations Lord
Beauport had gone, taking Lord Caterham with
him. The speeches and recitations were over,
and the crowd of spectators were filing out into

the quadrangle, when Lord Caterham, whose chair was being wheeled by a servant close by his father's side, heard a cheery voice say, "What, Brakespere! Gad, Lord Beauport, I mean! I forgot. Well, how are you, my dear fellow? I haven't seen you since we sat on the same form in that old place." Lord Caterham looked up and saw his father shaking hands with a jolly-looking middle-aged man, who rattled on—"Well, and you've been in luck and are a great gun! I'm delighted to hear it. You're just the fellow to bear your honours bravely. O yes, I'm wonderfully well, thank God. And I've got my boy here at the old shop, doing just as we used to do, Brakespere—Beauport, I mean. I'll introduce you. Here, Charley!" calling to him a fine handsome lad; "this is Lord Beauport, an old schoolfellow of mine. And you, Beauport,— you've got children, eh?"

"O yes," said Lord Beauport—"two boys."

"Ah! that's right. I wish they'd been here; I should have liked to have seen them." The man rattled on, but Lord Caterham heard no more. He had heard enough. He knew that his father was ashamed to acknowledge his maimed and crippled child—ashamed of a comparison between the stalwart son of his old schoolfellow and his own blighted lad; and that night Lord Caterham's pillow was wet with tears, and he prayed to God that his life might be taken from him.

Twice since then the same feelings had been violently excited; but the sense of his position, the knowledge that he was a perpetual grief and affliction to his parents, was ever present, and pervaded his very being. To tell truth, neither his father nor his mother ever outwardly manifested their disappointment or their sorrow at the hopeless physical state of their firstborn son; but Lord Caterham read his father's trouble in thousands of covert glances thrown towards the occupant of the wheeled chair, which the elder man thought were all unmarked, in short self-suppressed sighs, in sudden shiftings of the conversation when any subject involving a question of physical activity or muscular force happened to be touched upon, in the persistent way in which his father excluded him from those regular solemn festivities of the season, held at certain special times, and at which he by right should certainly have been present.

No man knew better than Lord Beauport the horrible injustice he was committing ; he felt that he was mutely rebelling· against the decrees of Providence, and adding to the affliction already mysteriously dispensed to his unfortunate son by his treatment. He fought against it, but without avail; he *could* not bow his head and kiss the rod by which he had been smitten. Had his heir been brainless, dissipated, even bad, he could have forgiven him. He did in his heart forgive his second son when he became all three ; but that he, George Brakespere, handsome Brakespere, one of the best athletes of the day, should have to own that poor misshapen man as his son and heir!—it was too much. He tried to persuade himself that he loved his son; but he never looked at him without a shudder, never spoke of him with unflushed cheeks.

As for Lady Beauport, from the time that the child's malady first was proclaimed incurable, she never took the smallest interest in him, but devoted herself, as much as devotion was compatible with perpetual attendance at ball, concert, and theatre, to her second son. As a child, Lord Caterham had, by her express commands, been studiously kept out of her sight; and now that he was a man, she saw very much less of him than of many strangers. A dozen times in the year she would enter his room and remain a few minutes, asking for his taste in a matter of fancy-costume, or something of the kind; and then she would brush his forehead with her lips, and rustle away perfectly satisfied with her manner of discharging the duties of maternity.

And Lord Caterham knew all this; read it as in a book; and suffered, and was strong. Who know most of life, discern character most readily, and read it most deeply? We who what we call "mix in the world," hurry hither and thither, buffeting our way through friends and foes, taking the rough and the smooth, smiling here, frowning there, but ever pushing onward? Or the quiet ones, who lie by in the nooks and lanes, and look on at the strife, and mark the quality and effect of the blows struck; who see not merely how, but why the battle has been undertaken, who can trace the strong and weak points of the attack and defence, see the skirmishers thrown out here, the feigned retreat there, the mine ready prepared in the far distance? How many years had that crippled man looked on at life, standing as it were at the gates and peering in at the antics and dalliances, the bowings and scrapings, the mad moppings and idiotic mowings of the puppets performing? And had he not arrived during this period at a perfect knowledge of how the wires were pulled, and what was the result?

Among them but not of them, in the midst of the whirl of London but as isolated as a hermit, with keen analytical powers, and leisure and opportunity to give them full swing, Lord Caterham passed his life in studying the lives of other people, in taking off the padding and the drapery,

the paint and the tinsel, in looking behind the
grins, and studying the motives for the sneers.
Ah, what a life for a man to pass! situated as
Lord Caterham was, he must under such circum-
stances have become either a Quilp or an angel.
The natural tendency is to the former: but
Providence had been kind in one instance to Lord
Caterham, and he, like Mr. Disraeli, went in for
the angel.

His flow of spirits was generally, to say the
least of it, equable. When the dark hour was
on him he suffered dreadfully; but this morning
he was more than usually low, for he had been
pondering over his brother's insane downfall, and
it was with something like real pleasure that he
heard his servant announce "Mr. Barford," and
gave orders for that gentleman's admittance.

The Honourable Algernon Barford by prescrip-
tive right, but "Algy Barford" to any one after
two days' acquaintance with him, was one of
those men whom it is impossible not to call by
their Christian names; whom it is impossible
not to like as an acquaintance; whom it is diffi-

cult to take into intimate friendship; but with whom no one ever quarrelled. A big, broad-chested, broad-faced, light-whiskered man, perfectly dressed, with an easy rolling walk, a pleasant presence, a way of enarming and "old boy-ing" you, without the least appearance of undue familiarity; on the contrary, with a sense of real delight in your society; with a voice which, without being in the least affected, or in the remotest degree resembling the tone of the stage-nobleman, had the real swell ring and roll in it; a kindly, sunny, chirpy, world-citizen, who, with what was supposed to be a very small income, lived in the best society, never borrowed or owed a sovereign, and was nearly always in good temper. Algy Barford was the very man to visit you when you were out of spirits. A glance at him was cheering; it revived one at once to look at his shiny bald forehead fringed with thin golden hair, at his saucy blue eyes, his big grinning mouth furnished with sparkling teeth; and when he spoke, his voice came ringing out with a cheery music of its own.

"Hallo, Caterham!" said he, coming up to the chair and placing one of his big hands on the occupant's small shoulder; "how goes it, my boy? Wanted to see you, and have a chat. How are you, old fellow, eh? Where does one put one's hat, by the way, dear old boy? Can't put it under my seat, you know, or I should think I was in church; and there's no place in this den of yours; and—ah, that'll do, on that lady's head. Who is it? O, Pallas Athené; ah, very well then, *non invitâ Minervâ*, she'll support my castor for me. Fancy my recollecting Latin, eh? but I think I must have seen it on somebody's crest. Well, and now, old boy, how are you?"

"Well, not very brilliant this morning, Algy. I—"

"Ah, like me, got rats, haven't you?"

"Rats?"

"Yes; whenever I'm out of spirits I think I've got rats—sometimes boiled rats. O, it's all very well for you to laugh, Caterham; but you know, though I'm generally pretty jolly, some-

times I have a regular file-gnawing time of it.
I think I'll take a peg, dear old boy—a sherry
peg—just to keep me up."

"To be sure. Just ring for Stevens, will you?
he'll—"

"Not at all; I recollect where the sherry is
and where the glasses live. *Nourri dans le sérail,
j'en connais les détours.* Here they are. Have a
peg, Caterham?"

"No, thanks, Algy; the doctor forbids me
that sort of thing. I take no exercise to carry it
off, you know; but I thought some one told me
you had turned teetotaller."

"Gad, how extraordinarily things get wind,
don't you know! So I did, honour!—kept to it
all strictly, give you my word, for—ay, for a
fortnight; but then I thought I might as well
die a natural death, so I took to it again.
This is the second peg I've had to-day—took
number one at the Foreign Office, with my
cousin Jack Lambert. You know Jack?—
little fellow, short and dirty, like a winter's
day."

" I know him," said Caterham, smiling; " a sharp fellow."

" O yes, deuced cute little dog—knows every thing. I wanted him to recommend me a new servant—obliged to send my man away—couldn't stand him any longer—always worrying me."

" I thought he was a capital servant?"

" Ye-es; knew too much though, and went to too many evening-parties—never would give me a chance of wearing my own black bags and dress-boots—kept 'em in constant requisition, by Jove! A greedy fellow too. I used to let him get just outside the door with the breakfast-things, and then suddenly call him back; and he never showed up without his mouth full of kidney, or whatever it was. And he always would read my letters—before I'd done with them, I mean. I'm short-sighted, you know, and obliged to get close to the light: he was in such a hurry to find out what they were about, that he used to peep in through the window, and read them over my shoulder. I found this out; and this morning I was ready for him with my fist neatly doubled-up in a thick towel. I saw his shadow come stealing across the paper, and then I turned round and let out at him slap through the glass. It was a gentle hint that I had spotted his game; and so he came in when he had got his face right, and begged me to suit myself in a month, as he had heard of a place which he thought he should like better. Now, can you tell me of any handy fellow, Caterham?"

"Not I; I'm all unlikely to know of such people. Stay, there was a man that—"

"Yes; and then you stop. Gad, you are like the rest of the world, old fellow: you have an *arrière pensée* which prevents your telling a fellow a good thing."

"No, not that, Algy. I was going to say that there was a man who was Lionel's servant. I don't know whether he has got another place; but Lionel, you know—" and Lord Caterham stopped with a knot in his throat and burning cheeks.

"I know, dear old boy," said Algy Barford, rising from his seat and again placing his hand on Caterham's shoulder; "of course I know. You're too much a man of the world"—(Heaven help us! Caterham a man of the world! But this was Algy Barford's pleasant way of putting it)—"not to know that the clubs rang with the whole story last night. Don't shrink, old boy. It's a bad business; but I never heard such tremendous sympathy expressed for a—for a buffer— as for Lionel. Every body says he must have been no end cornered before he—before he—well, there's no use talking of it. But what I wanted to say to you is this,—and I'm deuced glad you mentioned Lionel's name, old fellow, for I've been thinking all the time I've been here how I could bring it in. Look here! he and I were no end chums, you know; I was much older than he; but we took to each other like any thing, and— and I got a letter from him from Liverpool with— with an enclosure for you, old boy."

Algy Barford unbuttoned his coat as he said these last words, took a long breath, and seemed immensely relieved, though he still looked anxiously towards his friend.

"An enclosure for me?" said Lord Caterham, turning deadly white; "no further trouble—no further misery for—"

"On my honour, Caterham, I don't know what it is," said Algy Barford; "he doesn't hint it in his letter to me. He simply says, 'Let the enclosed be given to Caterham, and given by your own hand.' He underlines that last sentence; and so I brought it on. I'm a bungling jackass, or I should have found means to explain it myself, by Jove! But as you have helped me, so much the better."

"Have you it with you?"

"O yes; brought it on purpose," said Algy, rising and taking his coat from a chair, and his hat from the head of Pallas Athené; "here it is. I don't suppose any thing from poor Lionel can be very brilliant just now; but still, I know nothing. Good-by, Caterham, old fellow; can't help me to a servant-man, eh? See you next week; meantime,—and this earnest, old boy,—if there's any thing I can do to help Lionel in any shape, you'll let me know, won't you, old fellow?"

And Algy Barford handed Lord Caterham the letter, kissed his hand, and departed in his usual airy, cheery fashion.

That night Lord Caterham did not appear at the dinner-table; and his servant, on being asked, said that his master "had been more than usual queer-like," and had gone to bed very early.

CHAPTER VI.

GEOFFREY LUDLOW was in his way a recognisant
and a grateful man, grateful for such mercies
as he knew he enjoyed; but from never having
experienced its loss, he was not sufficiently appre-
ciative of one of the greatest of life's blessings, the
faculty of sleep at will. He could have slept, had
he so willed it, under .the tremendous cannon-
ading, the *feu-d'enfer*, before Sebastopol, or while
Mr. Gladstone was speaking his best speech, or
Mr. Tennyson was reading aloud his own poetry;
whenever and wherever he chose he could sleep
the calm peaceful sleep of an infant. Some people
tell you they are too tired to sleep—that was never
the case with Geoffrey; others that their minds
are too full, that they are too excited, that the
weather is too hot or too cold, that there is too

much noise, or that the very silence is too oppres-
sive. But, excited or comatose, hot or cold, in
the rumble of London streets or the dead silence
of—well, he had never tried the Desert, but let
us say Walton-on-the-Naze, Geoffrey Ludlow no
sooner laid his head on the pillow than he went off
into a sound, glorious, healthy sleep—steady, calm,
and peaceful; not one of your stertorous, heavy,
growling slumbers, nor your starting, fly-catching,
open-mouthed, moaning states, but a placid, regular sleep, so quiet and undisturbed that he scarcely
seemed to breathe; and often as a child had caused
his mother to examine with anxiety whether the
motionless figure stretched upon the little bed was
only sleeping naturally, or whether the last long
sleep had not fallen on it.

Dreams he had, no doubt; but they by no
means disturbed the refreshing, invigorating character of his repose. On the night of his adventure in the streets, he dreamt the Lamia dream
without its in the least affecting his slumber; and
when he opened his eyes the next morning, with
the recollection of where he was, and what day it

was, and what he had to do—those post-waking
thoughts which come to all of us—there came upon
him an indefinable sensation of something pleasurable and happy, of something bright and sunshiny, of something which made his heart feel
light within him, and caused him to open his
eyes and grapple with the day at once.

Some one surely must long ere this have remarked how our manner of waking from slumber
is affected by our state of mind. The instant that
consciousness comes upon us, the dominant object of our thoughts, be it pleasant or horrible,
is before us: the absurd quarrel with the man
in the black beard last night, about—what *was*
it about? the acceptance which Smith holds,
which must be met, and can't be renewed; the
proposal in the conservatory to Emily Fairbairn,
while she was flushed with the first *valse* after
supper, and we with Mrs. Tresillian's cham-
pagne;—or, *per contra*, as they say in the City,
the thrilling pressure of Flora Maitland's hand,
and the low whisper in which she gave us ren-
dezvous at the Botanical Fête this afternoon; the

lawyer's letter informing us of our godfather's
handsome legacy;—all these, whether for good
or ill, come before us with the first unclosing of
our eyelids. If agreeable we rouse ourselves at
once, and lie simultaneously chewing the cud of
pleasant thoughts and enjoying the calm haven
of our bed; if objectionable, we try and shut
them out yet for a little while, and turning round
court sleep once more.

What was the first thought that flashed
across Geoffrey Ludlow's brain immediately on
his waking, and filled him with hope and joy?
Not the remembrance of the purchase of his
picture by Mr. Stompff, though that certainly
occurred to him, with Stompff's promises of future employment, and the kind words of his old
friends at the Titians, all floating simultaneously
across his mind. But with these thoughts came
the recollection of a fragile form, and a thin
hand with long lithe fingers wound round his
own, and a low feeble voice whispering the
words " Bless you!—saved me!" in his listening
ear.

Beneath the flickering gas-lamps, or in the dim half-light of Mrs. Flexor's room, he had been unable to make out the colour of the eyes, or of the thick hair which hung in heavy masses over her cheeks; it was a spiritual recollection of her at the best; but he would soon change that into a material inspection. So, after settling in his own mind—that mind which coincides so readily with our wishes—that it was benevolence which prompted his every action, and which roused in him the desire to know how the patient of the previous night was getting on, he sprang from his bed, and pulled the string of his shower-bath with an energy which not even the knowledge of the water's probable temperature could mitigate. But he had not proceeded half-way through his toilet, when the old spirit of irresolution began to exercise its dominion over him. Was it not somewhat of a Quixotic adventure in which he was engaging? To succour a starving frozen girl on a wet night was merely charitable and humane; there was no man of any thing like decent feeling

but would have acted as he had done, and
—by George!—here the hair-brushes were sus-
pended in mid-air, just threatening a descent
one on either side of his bushy head—wouldn't
it have been better to have accepted Charley
Potts's suggestion, and let the policeman take
her to the workhouse? There she would have
had every attention and— bah! every attention!
the truckle-bed in a gaunt bare room, surrounded
by disease in every shape; the prefunctory visits
of the parish-doctor; the—O no! and, moreover,
had he not heard, or at all events imagined he
heard, the pallid lips mutter "Not there!" No!
there was something in her which—which—at all
events—well, *ruat cœlum*, it was done, and he
must take the consequences; and down came the
two hair-brushes like two avalanches, and worried
his unresisting scalp like two steam-harrows.
The recollection of the fragile frame, and the
thin hands, and the broken voice, supported by
the benevolent theory, had it all their own way
from that time out, until he had finished dressing,
and sent him downstairs in a happy mood, pleased

with what he had done, more pleased still with
the notion of what he was about to do. He entered
the room briskly, and striding up to an old lady
sitting at the head of the breakfast-table, gave
her a sounding kiss.

"Good-morning, dearest mother.—How do,
Til dear?" turning to a young woman who was
engaged in pouring out the tea. "I'm late again,
I see."

"Always on sausage mornings, I notice, Geoffrey," said Mrs. Ludlow, with a little asperity. "It
does not so much matter with haddock, though it
becomes leathery; or eggs, for you like them hard;
but sausages should be eaten hot, or not at all;
and to-day, when I'd sent specially for these,
knowing that nasty herb-stuffing is indigestible—
let them deny it if they can—it does seem hard
that—well, never mind—"

Mrs. Ludlow was a very good old lady, with
one great failing: she was under the notion that
she had to bear what she called "a cross," a
most uncomfortable typical object, which caused
all her friends the greatest annoyance, but in

which, though outwardly mournful, she secretly
rejoiced, as giving her a peculiar status in her
circle. This cross intruded itself into all the
social and domestic details of her life, and was
lugged out metaphorically on all possible occasions.

"Don't mind me, mother," said Geoff; "the
sausages will do splendidly. I overslept myself;
I was a little late last night."

"O, at those everlasting Titians.—I declare I
forgot," said the young woman who had been
addressed as "Til," and who was Geoffrey's only
sister. "Ah, poor fellow! studying his art till
two this morning, wasn't he?" And Miss Til
made a comic sympathetic *moue*, which made
Geoff laugh.

"Two!" said Mrs. Ludlow; "nearer three,
Matilda. I ought to know, for I had water running down my back all night, and my feet as
cold as stone; and I had a perfect recollection of
having left the key of the linen-closet in the
door, owing to my having been hurried down to
luncheon yesterday when I was giving Martha out

the clean pillow-cases. However, if burglars do break into that linen-closet, it won't be for my not having mentioned it, as I call you to witness, Matilda."

"All right, mother," said Geoffrey; "we'll run the risk of that. I'm very sorry I disturbed the house, but I *was* late, I confess; but I did some good, though."

"O yes, Geoffrey, we know," said Matilda. "Got some new notions for a subject, or heard some æsthetic criticism; or met some wonderful lion, who's going to astonish the world, and of whom no one ever hears again! You always have done something extraordinary when you're out very late, I find."

"Well, I did something really extraordinary last night. I sold my picture the 'Ballroom,' you know; and for what do you think?—two hundred pounds."

"O, Geoff, you dear, darling old Geoff! I am so glad! Two hundred pounds! O, Geoff, Geoff! You dear, lucky old fellow!" and Miss Til flung her arms round her brother's neck and

hugged him with delight. Mrs. Ludlow said never
a word; but her cross melted away momentarily,
her eyes filled with tears, and her lips quivered.
Geoffrey noticed this, and so soon as he had
returned his sister's hearty embrace, he went up
to his mother, and kneeling by her side, put up
his face for her kiss.

".God bless you, my son!" said the old lady
reverently, as she gave it; " God bless you! This
is brave news, indeed. I knew it would come in
time; but—"

"Yes; but tell us all about it, Geoff. How
did it come about? and however did you pluck
up courage, you dear, bashful, nervous old thing,
to ask such a price?"

" I—why, Til, you know that I—and you, dear
mother, you know too that—not that I am bashful,
as Til says; but still there's something. O, I should
never have sold the picture, I believe, if I'd been let
alone. It was Charley Potts sold it for me."

" Charles Potts! That ridiculous young man!
Well, I should never have thought it," said Mrs.
Ludlow.

Miss Matilda said nothing, but a faint flush rose on her neck and cheeks, and died away again as quickly as it came.

"O, he's a capital man of business—for any body else, that's to say. He don't do much good for himself. He sold the picture for me, and prevented my saying a word in the whole affair. And who do you think has bought it? Mr. Stompff the great dealer, who tells me he'll take as many more of the same style as I like to paint."

"This is great news indeed, my boy," said the old lady. "You've only to persevere, and your fortune's made. Only one thing, Geoffrey, —never paint on Sunday, or you'll never become a great man."

"Well but, mother," said Geoff, smiling, "Sir Joshua Reynolds painted always on Sundays until Johnson's death; and he was a great man."

"Ah, well, my dear," replied his mother forcibly, if not logically, "that's nothing to do with it."

Then Geoffrey, who had been hurrying through

his sausage, and towards the last began to grow
nervous and fidgety—accounted for by his mother
and sister from his anxiety to go and see Mr.
Stompff, and at once fling himself on to fresh
canvases—finished his breakfast, and went out to
get his hat.   Mrs. Ludlow, with her "cross"
rapidly coming upon her, sat down to "do the
books,"—an inspection of the household brigade
of tradesmen's accounts which she carried on
weekly with the sternest rigour; and Matilda, who
was by no means either a romantic or a strong-
minded woman, commenced to darn a basketful of
Geoffrey's socks.   Then the sock-destroyer put
his head in at the door, his mouth ornamented
with a large cigar, and calling out "Good-by,"
departed on his way.

The fragile form, the thin hands, and the soft
low voice had it all their own way with Geoffrey
Ludlow now.   He was going to see their owner;
in less than an hour he should know the colour of
the eyes and the hair; and figuratively Geoffrey
walked upon air; literally, he strode along with
bright eyes and flushed cheeks, swinging his stick,

and, but for the necessity of clenching his cigar between his teeth, inclined to hum a tune aloud. He scarcely noticed any of the people he met; but such as he did casually glance at he pitied from the bottom of his soul: there were no thin hands or soft voices waiting for them. And it must be owned that the passers-by who noticed him returned his pity. The clerks on the omnibuses, sucking solemnly at their brier-root pipes, or immersed in their newspapers, solemn staid men going in "to business," on their regular daily routine, looked up with wonder on this buoyant figure, with its black wideawake hat and long floating beard, its jerky walk, its swinging stick, and its general air of light-hearted happiness. The cynical clerks, men with large families, whom nothing but an increase of salary could rouse, interchanged shoulder-shrugs of contempt, and the omnibus-conductor, likewise a cynic, after taking a long stare at Geoffrey, called out to his driver, "'Appy cove that! looks as if he'd found a fourpenny-piece, don't he?"

. Entirely ignorant of the attention he was at

tracting, Geoff blithely pursued his way. He lived at Brompton, and he was bound for the neighbourhood of Portland Place; so he turned in at the Albert Gate, and crossing the enclosure and the Row, made for Grosvenor Gate. In the Park he was equally the object of remark: the nurse-girls called their charges to come "to heel" out of the way of that "nasty ugly big man;" the valetudinarians taking their constitutional in the Row loathed him for swinging his stick and making their horses shy as he passed; the park-keepers watched him narrowly, as one probably with felonious intent to the plants or the ducks.

Still, utterly unconscious, Geoffrey went swinging along across Grosvenor Square, down Brook Street; and not until he turned into Bond Street did he begin to realise entirely the step he was about to take. Then he wavered, in mind and in gait; he thought he would turn back; he did turn back, irresolute, doubtful. Better have nothing more to do with it; nip it in the bud; send Charley Potts with a couple of sovereigns to Mrs. Flexor's, and tell her to set the girl on her way again, and wish her God-speed. But what if she were still ill, unable to move? people didn't gain sufficient strength in twelve hours; and Charley, though kind-hearted, was rather *brusque;* and then the low voice, with the "Bless you!—saved me!" came murmuring in his ear; and Geoffrey, like Whittington, turned again, and strode on towards Little Flotsam Street.

When he got near Flexor's door, he faltered again, and very nearly gave in : but looking up, saw Mrs. Flexor standing on the pavement; and perceiving by her manner that his advent had been noticed, proceeded, and was soon alongside that matron.

" Good-morning, Mrs. Flexor."

" Good-mornin', sir; thought you'd be over early, though not lookin' for you now, but for Reg'las, my youngest plague, so called after Mr. Scumble's Wictory of the Carthageniums, who has gone for milk for some posset for our dear; who is much better this mornin', the Lord a mussy! Dr. Rollix have been, and says we may sit up a little, if taking nourishment prescribed;

and pleased to see you we shall be. A pretty creetur, Mr. Ludlow, though thin as thin and low as low: but what can we expect?"

" She is better, then ?"

" A deal better, more herself like ; though not knowing what she was before, I can't exactly say. Flexor was fine and buffy when he came home last night, after you was gone, sir. Them nasty Titiums, he always gets upset there. And now he's gone to sit to Mr. Potts for—ah, well, some Roman party whose name I never can remember."

" Is your patient up, Mrs. Flexor ?"

" Gettin'. We shall be ready to see you in five minutes, sir. I'll go and see to her at once."

Mrs. Flexor retired, and Geoffrey was left to himself for a quarter of an hour standing in the street, during which time he amused himself as most people would under similar circumstances. That is to say, he stared at the houses opposite and at the people who passed; and then he beat his stick against his leg, and then he whistled a tune, and then, having looked at his watch five times, he looked at it for the sixth. Then he walked up the street, taking care to place his foot on the round iron of every coal-shoot; and then he walked down the street, carrying out a determination to step in the exact centre of every flagstone; and then, after he had pulled his beard a dozen times, and lifted his wideawake hat as many, that the air might blow upon his hot forehead, he saw Mrs. Flexor's head protrude from the doorway, and he felt very much inclined to run away. But he checked himself in time, and entered the house, and, after a ghostly admonition from Mrs. Flexor "not to hagitate her," he opened the parlour-door, which Mrs. Flexor duly shut behind him, and entered the room.

Little light ever groped its way between the closely-packed rows of houses in Little Flotsam Street, even on the brightest summer day; and on a dark and dreary winter's morning Mrs. Flexor's little front parlour was horribly dark. The worthy landlady had some wild notion, whence derived no one knew, that an immense amount of gentility

was derived from keeping the light out; and consequently the bottom part of her windows were
fitted with dwarf wire-blinds, and the top part
with long linen-blinds, and across both were
drawn curtains made of a kind of white fishing-
net; so that even so little daylight as Little
Flotsam Street enjoyed was greatly diluted in the
Flexorian establishment.

But Geoffrey Ludlow saw stretched out on a
miserable black horsehair sofa before him there
this fragile form which had been haunting his
brain for the last twelve hours. Ah, how thin and
fragile it was; how small it looked, even in its
worn draggled black-merino dress! As he advanced noiselessly, he saw that the patient slept;
her head was thrown back, her delicate white
hands (and almost involuntarily Geoffrey remarked
that she wore no wedding-ring) were clasped
across her breast, and her hair, put off her dead-
white face, fell in thick clusters over her shoulders.

With a professional eye Geoffrey saw at once
that whatever trouble she might have taken, she
could not have been more artistically posed than

in this natural attitude. The expression of her
eyes was wanting; and, as he sunk into a chair at
her feet, her eyes opened upon him. Then he saw
her face in its entirety; saw large deep-violet
eyes, with dark lashes and eyebrows; a thin,
slightly aquiline nose; small thin close lips, and a
little chin; a complexion of the deadest white,
without the smallest colour; and hair, long thick
rich luxuriant hair, of a deep, red-gold colour—
not the poetic "auburn," not the vulgar " carrots;" a rich metallic red, unmistakable, admitting of no compromise, no darkening by grease
or confining by fixature—a great mass of deep-red
hair, strange, weird, and oddly beautiful. The
deep-violet eyes, opening slowly, fixed their regard on his face without a tremor, and with a
somewhat languid gaze; then brightening slowly,
while the hands were unclasped, and the voice—
how well Geoff remembered its tones, and how
they thrilled him again!—murmured faintly, " It
is you!"

What is that wonderful something in the human
voice which at once proclaims the social status of

the speaker? The proletary and the *roturier*, Nature willing, can have as good features, grow as flowing beards, be as good in stature, grace, and agility, as the noblest patrician, or the man in whose veins flows the purest *sangre azul;* but they fail generally in hands, always in voice. Geoffrey Ludlow, all his weakness and irresolution notwithstanding, was necessarily by his art a student of life and character; and no sooner did he hear those three little words spoken in that tone, than all his floating ideas of shamming tramp or hypocritical street-walker, as connected with the recipient of his last night's charity, died away, and he recognised at once the soft modulations of education, if not of birth.

But those three words, spoken in deep low quivering tones, while they set the blood dancing in Geoffrey Ludlow's veins, made him at the same time very uncomfortable. He had a dread of any thing romantic; and there flashed through his mind an idea that he could only answer this remark by exclaiming, "'Tis I!" or "Ay, indeed!" or something else equally absurd and ridiculous. So he contented himself with bowing his head and putting out his hand—into which the long lithe fingers came fluttering instantly. Then with burning cheeks Geoffrey bent forward, and said, " You are better to-day ?"

" O, so much — so much better! thanks to you, thanks to you !"

" Your doctor has been ?" She bowed her head in reply.

" And you have every thing you wish for ?" She bowed again, this time glancing up—with, O, such a light in the deep-violet eyes—into Geoffrey's face !

" Then—then I will leave you now," said he, awkwardly enough. The glance fell as he said this; but flashed again full and earnest in an instant; the lithe fingers wound round his wrist, and the voice, even lower and more tremulously than before, whispered, " You'll come to-morrow ?"

Geoff flushed again, stammered, " Yes, O, by all means !" made a clumsy bow, and went out.

Now this was a short, and not a particularly

satisfactory, interview; but the smallest detail of it remained in Geoffrey Ludlow's mind, and was reproduced throughout the remainder of that day and the first portion of the succeeding night, for him to ponder over. He felt the clasp of her fingers yet on his wrist, and he heard the soft voice, " You'll come to-morrow ?"   It must be a long distance, he thought, that he would not go to gaze into those eyes, to touch that hand, to hear that voice again !

CHAPTER VII.

Mr. Potts lived in Berners Street, on the second-floor of a rambling big old-fashioned house, which in its palmy days had been inhabited by people of distinction; and in which it was rumoured in the art-world that the great Mr. Fuseli had once lived, and painted those horrors which sprung from the nightmare consequent on heavy suppers of pork-chops. But these were the days of its decadence, and each of its floors had now a separate and distinct tenant. The ground-floor was a kind of half show-room, half-shop, held by Mr. Lectern, the great church-upholsterer. Specimens of stained-glass windows, croziers, and brass instruments like exaggerated beadles'-staves, gilt sets of communion-service, and splendidly-worked altar-cloths occupied the walls; the visitor walked up to the desk at which Mr. Lectern presided, between groves of elaborately-carved pulpits and reading-desks, and brazen eagles were extending their wings in every available corner. On the first-floor Mdlle. Stetti gave lessons to the nobility, gentry, and the public in general in the fashionable dances of the day, and in the Magyar sceptre-exercises for opening the chest and improving the figure. Mdlle. Stetti had a very large connection; and as many of her pupils were adults who had never learned to dance while they were supple and tender, and as, under the persevering tuition of their little instructress, they gambolled in a cumbrous and rather elephantine manner, they earned for themselves many hearty anathemas from Mr. Potts, who found it impossible to work with anything like a steady hand while the whole house was rocking under the influence of a stout stockbroker doing the "changes," or while the walls trembled at every bound of the fourteen-stone lady from Islington, who was being initiated into the mysteries of the gavotte. But Charley Potts's pipe was the only confidant of his growled anathemas, and on the whole he got on remarkably well with his neighbours; for Mr. Lectern had lent him bits of oak furniture to paint from; and once, when he was ill, Mdlle. Stetti, who was the dearest, cheeriest, hardest-working, best-tempered little creature in existence, had made him broths and "goodies" with her own hand, and when he was well, had always a kind word and a smile for him—and, indeed, revelled in the practical humour and buffoonery of "*ce farceur* Pott." For Mr. Potts was nothing if not funny; the staircase leading to his rooms began to be decorated immediately after you had passed Mdlle. Stetti's apartments; an enormous hand, sketched in crayon, with an outstretched finger, directed attention to an inscription—"To the halls of Potts!" Just above the little landing you were confronted by a big beefeater's head, out of the mouth of which floated a balloon-like legend—"Walk up, walk up, and see the great Potts!" The aperture of the letter-box in the door formed the mouth in a capital caricatured head of Charley himself; and instead of a bell-handle there hung a hare's-foot, beneath

which was gummed a paper label with a written
inscription—" Tug the trotter."

Three days after the gathering at the Titian
Sketching-Club, Mr. Potts sat in his studio, smoking a pipe, and glaring vacantly at a picture on
an easel in front of him.   It was not a comfortable room ; its owner's warmest friend could not
have asserted that.   There was no carpet, and the
floor was begrimed with the dirt of ages, and with
spilt tobacco and trodden-in cigar-ash.   The big
window was half stopped-up, and had no curtain.
An old oak-cabinet against the wall, surmounted
by the inevitable plaster torso, and studies of
hands and arms, had lost one of its supporting
feet, and looked as though momentarily about to
topple forward.   A table in the middle of the
room was crowded with litter, amongst which a
pewter-pot reared itself conspicuously.   Over an
old sofa were thrown a big rough Inverness-cape,
a wideawake hat, and a thick stick; while on a
broken, ragged, but theatrically-tawdry arm-chair,
by the easel, were a big palette already "set," a
colour-box, and a sheaf of brushes.   Mr. Potts

was dressed in a shepherd's-plaid shooting-coat,
adorned here and there with dabs of paint, and
with semi-burnt brown patches, the result of the
incautious dropping of incandescent tobacco and
vesuvians. He had on a pair of loose rough
trousers, red-morocco slippers without heels, and
he wore no neckcloth; but his big turned-down
shirt-collar was open at the throat. He wore no
beard, but had a large sweeping Austrian mous-
tache, which curled fiercely at the ends; had thin
brown hair, light blue eyes, and the freshest and
healthiest of complexions. No amount of late
hours, of drinking and smoking, could apparently
have any effect on this baby-skin; and under the
influence of cold water and yellow soap, both of
which he used in large quantities, he seemed
destined to remain—so far as his complexion was
concerned—"beautiful for ever,"—or at least until long after Madame Rachel's clients had seen
the worthlessness of pigments. Looking at him
as he sat there—his back bent nearly double, his
eyes fixed on his picture, his pipe fixed stiffly between his teeth, and his big bony hands clasped

in front of him—there was no mistaking him for
any thing but a gentleman; ill-dressed, slatternly,
if you like; but a true gentleman, every inch of
him.

The " trotter " outside being tugged with tremendous violence, roused him from his reverie,
and he got up and opened the door, saying, as he
did so, " Why didn't you ring? I would, if I'd
been you. You're in the bell-hanging line, I
should think, by the way you jerked my wire.
Hollo, Bowker, my boy! is it you? What's the
matter? Are you chivied by a dun on the staircase, or fainting for a pull at the pewter, that you
come with such a ring as that? Bring your body
in, old man; there's a wind here enough to shave
you."

Mr. Bowker preceded his friend into the
room, looked into the pewter-pot, drained it,
wiped his beard with a handkerchief, which he
took out of his hat, and said, in a solemn deep
voice: " Potts, my pipkin, how goes it?"

" Pretty well, old man, pretty well—considering the weather. And you?"

" Your William *se porte bien*. Hallo !" glancing at the easel, while he took a pipe from his
pocket and filled it from a jar on the table;
" hallo! something new! What's the subject?
Who is the Spanish party in tights? and what's
the venerable buffer in the clerical get-up of the
period putting out his hand about ?"

" O, it's a scene from *Gil Blas*, where the
Archbishop of Grenada discharges him, you know."

" No, I don't, and I don't want to hear; your
William, dear boy, has discovered that life is too
short to have any thing explained to him : if he
don't see it at first, he let's it pass. The young
party's right leg is out of drawing, my chick;
just give your William a bit of chalk. There—
not being a patient at the Orthopædic Hospital—
that's where his foot would come to. The crim-
son of the reverend gent's gown is about as bad as
any thing I've seen for a long time, dear boy.
Hand over the palette and brushes for two
minutes. Your William is a rum old skittle;
but if there's one thing he knows about, it is
colour." And Charley, who knew that, with all

his eccentricity, Mr. Bowker, or "your William," as he always spoke of himself, was a thorough master of his art, handed him what he required, and sat by watching him.

A fat bald-headed man with a grizzled beard, a large paunch and flat splay feet, badly dressed and not too clean, Mr. Bowker did not give one the idea of ever having been an "object of interest" to any one save the waiter at the tavern where he dined, or the tobacconist where he bought his Cavendish. But yet there had been a day when bright eyes grew brighter at his approach, tiny ears latticed with chestnut-hair had eagerly drunk-in the music of his voice, gentle hands had thrilled beneath his touch. He had bright blue eyes himself then, and long hair, and a slim figure. He was young Mr. Bowker, whose first pictures exhibited at Somerset House had made such a sensation, and who was so much noticed by Sir David Wilkie, and for whom Mr. Northcote prophesied such a future, and whom Mr. Fuseli called a "coot prave poy!" He was the young Mr. Bowker who was recommended by Sir Thomas Lawrence as drawing-master to the lovely young wife of old **Mr. Van Den Bosch**, the Dutch banker and financier long resident in London. He was " that scoundrel Bowker, sir," who, being wildly romantic, fell head-over-ears in love with his pupil; and finding that she was cruelly ill-treated by the old ruffian her husband, ran away with her to Spain, and by that rash act smashed-up his career and finally settled himself for ever. Old Van Den Bosch got a divorce, and died, leaving all his money to his nephews; and then William Bowker and the woman he had eloped with returned to England, to find himself universally shunned and condemned. His art was as good, nay a thousand times better than ever; but they would not hear of him at the Royal Academy now; would not receive his pictures; would not allow the mention of his name. Patrons turned their backs on him, debts accumulated, the woman for whom he had sacrificed every thing died,—penitent so far as she herself was concerned, but adoring her lover to the last, and calling down

blessings on him with her latest breath. And
then William Bowker strove no more, but accepted
his position and sunk into what he was, a kindly,
jolly, graceless vagabond, doing no harm, but
very little good. He had a little private money
on which he lived; and as time progressed, some
of his patrons, who found he painted splendidly
and cheaply, came back to him and gave him
commissions; but he never again attempted to
regain his status; and so long as he had enough
to supply his simple daily wants, seemed content.
He was a great favourite with some half-dozen
young men of Charley Potts's set, who had a real
love and regard for him, and was never so happy
as when helping them with advice and manual
assistance.

Charley watched him at his work, and saw
with delight the archbishop's robe gradually
growing all a-glow beneath the master's touch;
and then, to keep him in good-humour and
amused, began to talk, telling him a score of
anecdotes, and finally asking him if he'd heard
any thing of Tommy Smalt.

"Tommy Smalt, sir?" cried Bowker, in his cheery voice; "Tommy Smalt, sir, is in clover! Your William has been able to put Tommy on to a revenue of at least thirty shillings a-week. Tommy is now the right-hand man of Jacobs of Newman Street; and the best judges say that there are no Ostades, Jan Steens, or Gerard Dows like Tommy's."

"What do you mean?—copies?"

"Copies! no, sir; originals!"

"Originals!"

"Certainly! original Tenierses, of boors drinking; Wouvermans, not forgetting the white horse; or Jan Steens, with the never-failing episode;—all carefully painted by Tommy Smalt and his fellow-labourers! Ah, Jacobs is a wonderful man! There never was such a fellow; he sticks at nothing; and when he finds a man who can do his particular work, he keeps him in constant employment."

"Well, but is the imposition never detected? Don't the pictures look new?"

"Oh, most verdant of youths, of course not!

The painting is clobbered with liquorice-water; and the varnish is so prepared that it cracks at once; and the signature in the corner is always authentic; and there's a genuine look of cloudy vacancy and hopeless bankruptcy about the whole that stamps it at once to the connoisseur as the real thing. Tommy's doing a ' Youth's Head' by Rembrandt now, which ought to get him higher pay; it ought indeed. It's for a Manchester man. They're very hot about Rembrandts at Manchester."

" Well, you've put me up to a new wrinkle. And Jacobs lives by this?"

" Lives by it! ay, and lives like a prince too. Mrs. J. to fetch him every day in an open barouche, and coachman and footman in sky-blue livery, and all the little J.'s hanging over the carriage-doors, rendering Newman Street dark with the shadow of their noses. Lives by it! ay, and why not? There will always be fools in the world, thank Heaven!—or how should you and I get on, Charley, my boy?—and so long as people will spend money on what they know nothing about, for the sake of cutting-out their friends, gaining a spurious reputation for taste, or cutting a swell as 'patrons of the fine-arts,' — patrons indeed! that word nearly chokes me!—it's quite right that they should be pillaged and done. No man can love art in the same manner that he can love pancakes. He must know something about it, and have some appreciation of it. Now no man with the smallest knowledge of art would go to Jacobs; and so I say that the lords and railway-men and cotton-men who go there simply as a piece of duff—to buy pictures as they would carpets—are deuced well served out. There! your William has not talked so much as that in one breath for many a long day. The pewter's empty. Send for some more beer, and let's have a damp; my throat's as dry as a lime-burner's wig."

Charley Potts took up the pewter-measure, and going on to the landing outside the door, threw open the staircase-window, and gave a shrill whistle. This twice repeated had some effect; for a very much-be-ribboned young lady in the bar of the opposite public-house looked up, and nodded with great complaisance; and then Charley, having made a solemn bow, waved the empty quart-pot three times round his head. Two minutes afterwards a bare-headed youth, with his shirt-sleeves rolled up to his shoulders, crossed the road, carefully bearing a pasteboard hat-box, with which he entered the house, and which he delivered into Mr. Potts's hands.

"Good boy, Richard! never forget the hat-box; come for it this evening, and take back both the empty pewters in it.—It would never do, Bowker, my boy, to have beer—vulgar beer, sir—in its native pewter come into a respectable house like this. The pious parties, who buy their rattletraps and properties of old Lectern down below, would be scandalised; and poor little Mossoo woman Stetti would lose her swell connection. So Caroline and I—that's Caroline in the bar, with the puce-coloured ribbons—arranged this little dodge; and it answers first-rate."

"Ha—a!" said Mr. Bowker, putting down the tankard half-empty, and drawing a long

breath; " beer is to your William what what's-
his-name is to thingummy; which, being interpreted, means that he can't get on without it.
I never take a big pull at a pewter without
thinking of our Geoff. How is our Geoff?"

" Our Geoff is—hush! some one coming up-
stairs. What's to-day? Friday. The day I told
the tailor to call. Hush!"

The footsteps came creaking up the stairs until they stopped outside Charley Potts's door, on
which three peculiar blows were struck,—one
very loud, then two in rapid succession.

" A friend!" said Charley, going to the door
and opening it. " Pass, friend, and give the
countersign! Hallo, Flexor! is it you? I forgot
our appointment for this morning. Come in."

It was, indeed, the great model, who, fresh-
shaved, and with his hair neatly poodled under
his curly-brimmed hat, entered the room with a
swagger, which, when he perceived a stranger,
he allowed to subside into an elaborate bow.

" Now then, Flexor, get to work! we won't
mind my friend here; he knows all this sort of

game of old," said Charley; while Flexor began
to arrange himself into the position of the ex-
pelled secretary of the archbishop.

" Ay, and I know Mr. Flexor of old, that's
another thing!" said Bowker, with a deep chuc-
kle, expelling a huge puff of smoke.

" Do you, sir?" said Flexor, still rigid in the
Gil-Blas position, and never turning his head;
" maybe, sir; many gents knows Flexor."

" Yes; but many gents didn't know Flexor
five-and-twenty years ago, when he stood for
' Mercutio discoursing of Queen Mab.' "

" Lor' a mussy!" cried Flexor, forgetting all
about his duty, parting the smoke with his hand
and bending down to look into William's face.
" It's Mr. Bowker, and I ought to have knowed
him by the voice. And how are you, sir? hearty
you look, though you've got a paucity of nob-
thatch, and what 'air you 'ave is that gray, you
might be your own grandfather. Why, I haven't
seen you since you was gold-medallist at the
'Cademy, 'cept once when you come with
Mrs. ——"

"There, that'll do, Flexor! I'm alive still, you see; and so I see are you. And your wife, is she alive?"

"O yes, sir; but, Lord, how different from what you know'd her! None of your Wenuses, nor Dalilys, nor Nell Gwyns now! she's growed stout and cumbersome, and never sits 'cept some gent wants a Mrs. Primrose in that everlastin' Wicar, or a old woman a-scoldin' a gal because she wants to marry a pore cove, or somethin' in that line; and then I says, 'Well, Jane, you may as well earn a shillin' an hour as any one else,' I says."

"And you've been a model all these years, Flexor?"

"Well, no sir—off and on; but I've always come back to it. I was a actor for three years; did Grecian stators,—Ajax defyin' the lightnin'; Slave a-listenin' to conspirators; Boy a-sharpenin' his knife, and that game, you know, in a cirkiss. But I didn't like it; they're a low lot, them actors, with no feelin' for art. And then I was a gentleman's-servant; but that wouldn't do;

they do dam' and cuss their servants so, the gentlemen do, as I couldn't stand it; and I was a mute."

" A mute!—what, a funeral mute?"

" Yes, sir; black-job business; and wery good that is,—plenty of pleasant comp'ny and agreeable talk, and nice rides in the summer time on the 'earses to all the pleasant simmetries in the suburbs! But in the winter it's frightful! and my last job I was nearly killed. We had a job at 'Ampstead, in the debth of snow; and it was frightful cold on the top of the 'Eath. It was the party's good lady as was going to be interred, and the party himself were frightful near; in fact, a reg'lar screw. Well, me and my mate had been standin' outside the 'ouse-door with the banners in our 'ands for an hour, until we was so froze we could scarcely hold the banners. So I says, I won't stand no longer, I says; and I gev a soft rap, and told the servant we must have a drop of somethin' short, or we should be killed with cold. The servant goes and tells her master, and what do you think he says?

'Drink!' he says. 'Nonsense!' he says; '*if they're cold, let 'em jump about and warm 'emselves*,' he says. Fancy a couple of mutes with their banners in their 'ands a-jumpin' about outside the door just before the party was brought out! So that disgusted me, and I gev it up, and come back to the old game agen."

"Now, Flexor," said Charley, "if you've finished your biography, get back again."

"All right, sir!" and again Flexor became rigid, as the student of Santillane.

"What were we talking of when Flexor arrived? O, I remember; I was asking you about Geoff Ludlow. What of him?"

"Well, sir, Geoff Ludlow has made a thundering *coup* at last. The other night at the Titians he sold a picture to Stompff for two hundred pounds; more than that, Stompff promised him no end of commissions."

"That's first-rate! Your William pledges him!" and Mr. Bowker finished the stout.

"He'll want all he can make, gentlemen," said Flexor, who, seeing the pewter emptied, became cynical; "he'll want all he can make, if he goes on as he's doin' now."

"What do you mean?" asked Bowker.

"He's in love, Mr. Ludlow is; that's wot I mean. That party—you know, Mr. Potts—as you brought to our place that night—he's been to see her every day, he has; and my missis says, from what she 'ave seen and 'eard—well, that's neither 'ere nor there," said Flexor, checking himself abruptly as he remembered that the key-hole was the place whence Mrs. Flexor's information had been derived.

Charley Potts gave a loud whistle, and said, "The Devil!" then turning to Bowker, he was about to tell the story of the wet night's adventure, but William putting up his finger warningly, grunted out "*Nachher!*" and Charley, who understood German, ceased his chatter and went on with his painting.

When the sitting was over, and Flexor had departed, William Bowker returned to the subject, saying, "Now, Charley, tell your William all about this story of Geoff and his adventure."

Charley Potts narrated it circumstantially, Bowker sitting grimly by and puffing his pipe the while. When he had finished, Bowker never spoke for full five minutes; but his brow was knit, and his teeth clenched round his pipe. At length he said, " This is a bad business, so far as I see; a devilish bad business! If the girl were in Geoff's own station, or if he were younger, it wouldn't so much matter; but Geoff must be forty now, and at that age a man's deuced hard to turn from any thing he gets into his head. Well, we must wait and see. I'd rather it were you, Charley, by a mile; one might have some chance then. But you never think of any thing of that sort, eh?"

What made Charley Potts colour as he said, " Well—not in Geoff's line, at all events"?

William Bowker noticed the flush, and said ruefully, " Ah, I see! Always the way! Now let's go and get some beef, or something to eat: I'm hungry."

CHAPTER VIII.

Mr. FLEXOR was by nature mendacious; indeed his employers used pleasantly to remark, that when he did not lie, it was simply by accident; but in what he had mentioned to Charley Potts about Geoffrey Ludlow's visits to the nameless female then resident in his, Flexor's, house, he had merely spoken the truth. To be sure there had been an *arrière pensée* in his remark; the fact being that Flexor objected to matrimony as an institute amongst his patrons. He found that by an artist in a celibate state beer was oftener sent for, donations of cigars were more frequent, cupboards were more constantly unlocked, and irregularities of attendance on his part, consequent on the frivolities of the preceding night, were more easily overlooked, than when there was a lady to share confidences and keys, and to regard all models, both male and female, as "horrid creatures." But although Mr. Flexor had spoken somewhat disparagingly of Geoffrey's frequent visits, and had by his hints roused up a certain amount of suspicion in the breasts of Charley Potts and that grim old cynic William Bowker, he was himself far from knowing what real ground for apprehension existed, or how far matters had progressed, at least with one of the parties concerned.

For Geoffrey Ludlow was hard hit! In vain he attempted to argue with himself that all he had done, was doing, and might do, was but prompted by benevolence. A secret voice within him told him that his attempts at self-deceit were of the feeblest, and that, did he but dare to confess it, he knew that there was in this woman whom he had rescued from starvation an attraction more potent than he had ever yet submitted to. It was, it may be said, his duty to call and see how she was getting on, to learn that she wanted for nothing, to hear from her own lips that his orders

for her comfort had been obeyed; but it was not
his duty to sit watching jealously every glance of
her eye, every turn of her head, every motion of
her lithe fingers. It was *not* his duty to bear
away with him recollections of how she sat when
she said this or answered that; of the manner in
which, following a habit of hers, she would push
back the thick masses of her gleaming hair, and
tuck them away behind her pretty ears; or, following another habit, she would drum petulantly
on the floor with her little foot, when talking of
any thing that annoyed her—as, for instance,
Mrs. Flexor's prying curiosity.

What was it that caused him to lie awake at
night, tossing from side to side on his hot pillow,
ever before him the deep-violet eyes, the pallid
face set in masses of deep-red hair, the slight frail
figure? What was it that made his heart beat
loudly, his breath come thickly, his whole being
tingle with a strange sensation—now ecstatic delight, now dull blank misery? Not philanthropy,
I trow. The superintendents of boys' reforma-
tories and refuges for the houseless poor may, in

thinking over what good they have achieved,
enjoy a comfortable amount of self-satisfaction
and proper pride; but I doubt if the feeling ever
rises to this level of excitement. Not much wonder if Geoffrey himself, suffering acutely under
the disease, knew not, or refused to avow to
himself, any knowledge of the symptoms. Your
darling child, peacefully sleeping in his little bed,
shall show here and there an angry skin-spot,
which you think heat or cold, or any thing else,
until the experienced doctor arrives, and with a
glance pronounces it scarlet-fever. Let us be
thankful, in such a case, that the prostrate patient
is young. Geoffrey's was as dire a malady, and
one which, coming on at forty years of age,
usually places the sufferer in a perilous state. It
was called Love; not the ordinary sober inclination of a middle-aged man, not that thin line of
fire quivering amongst a heap of ashes which be-
tokens the faded passion of the worn and sated
voluptuary; this was boy-love, calf-love, mad-
spooniness—any thing by which you can express
the silliest, wildest, pleasantest, most miserable

phase of human existence. It never comes but once to any one. The *caprices* of the voluptuary are as like to each other as peas or grains of sand ; the platonic attachments or the sentimental *liaisons* indulged in by foolish persons of both sexes with nothing to do may have some slight shade of distinction, but are equally wanting in backbone and *vis.* Not to man or woman is it given to be ever twice " in love "—a simple phrase, which means every thing, but needs very little explanation. My readers will comprehend what I want to convey, and will not require my feeble efforts in depicting the state. Suffice it to say, that Geoffrey Ludlow, who had hitherto gone through life scot-free, not because he was case-hardened, not because he was infection-proof, or that he had run no risks, but simply from the merest chance,— now fell a victim to the disease, and dropped powerless before its attack.

He did not even strive to make head against it much. A little of his constitutional wavering and doubtfulness came into play for a short time, suggesting that this passion—for such he must allow

it—was decidedly an unworthy one; that at present he knew nothing of the girl's antecedents;
and that her actual state did not promise much for
all she had to tell of what had gone before. At
certain times too, when things present themselves
in their least-roseate garb, notably on waking in
the morning, for instance, he allowed, to himself,
that he was making a fool of himself; but the
confidence extended no farther. And then, as the
day grew, and the sun came out, and he touched-
up his picture, and thought of the commissions
Mr. Stompff had promised him, he became
brighter and more hopeful, and he allowed his
thoughts to feast on the figure then awaiting him
in Little Flotsam Street, and he put by his sheaf
of brushes and his palette, and went up and exa-
mined himself in the glass over the mantelpiece.
He had caught himself doing this very frequently
within the last few days, and, half-chuckling inwardly, had acknowledged that it was a bad sign.
But though he laughed, he tweaked out the most
prominent gray hairs in his beard, and gave his
necktie a more knowing twist, and removed the

dabs of stray paint from his shooting-coat. Straws thrown up show which way the wind blows, and even such little sacrifices to vanity as these were in Geoffrey Ludlow very strong signs indeed.

He had paid three visits to Little Flotsam Street; and on the fourth morning, after a very poor pretence of work, he was at the looking-glass settling himself preparatory to again setting out. Ever since that midnight adventure after the Titians meeting, Geoffrey had felt it impossible to take his usual daily spell at the easel, had not done five-pounds worth of real work in the whole time, had sketched-in and taken-out, and pottered, and smoked over his canvas, perfectly conscious that he was doing no good, utterly unable to do any better. On this fourth morning he had been even more unsuccessful than usual; he was highly nervous; he could not even set his palette properly, and by no manner of means could he apply his thoughts to his work. He had had a bad night; that is, he had woke with a feeling that this kind of penny-journal romance, wherein a man finds a starving girl in the streets and falls desperately in love with her, could go on no longer in London and in the nineteenth century. She was better now, probably strong enough to get about ; he would learn her history, so much of it at least as she liked to tell; and putting her in some way of earning an honest livelihood, take his leave of her, and dismiss her from his thoughts.

He arrived at this determination in his studio ; he kept it as he walked through the streets; he wavered horribly when he came within sight of the door; and by the time he knocked he had resolved to let matters take their chance, and to act as occasion might suggest. It was not Mrs. Flexor who opened the door to him, but that worthy woman's youngest plague, Reg'las, who, with a brown eruption produced by liquorice round his lips, nodded his head, and calmly invited the visitor, as he would have done any one else, to "go up 'tairs." Geoffrey entered, patted the boy's head, and stopped at the parlour-door, at which he gave a low rap, and immediately turning the handle walked in.

She was lying as usual on the sofa immediately opposite the door; but what he had never
seen before, her hair was freed from the confining
comb, and was hanging in full luxuriance over
her shoulders. Great heavens, how beautiful she
looked! There had been a certain piquancy and
chic in her appearance when her hair had been
taken saucily off her face and behind her ears;
but they were nothing as compared to the pro-
found expression of calm holy resignation in that
dead-white face, set in that deep dead-gold frame
of hair. Geoff started when he saw it; was it a
Madonna of Raphael's, or a St. Teresa of Guido's,
which flashed across his mind? And as he looked
she raised her eyes, and a soft rosy flush spread
over her face, and melted as quickly as it came.
He seated himself on a chair by her side as usual,
and took her hand as usual, the blood tingling in
his fingers as he touched hers—as usual. She
was the first to speak.

"You are very early this morning. I scarcely
expected you so soon—as you may see;" and with
a renewed flush she took up the ends of her hair,

and was about to twist them up, when Geoffrey stopped her.

" Leave it as it is," said he in a low tone ; " it could not be better; leave it as it is."

She looked at him as he spoke; not a full straight glance, but through half-closed lids ; a prolonged gaze,—half-dreamy, half-intense; then released her hair, and let it again fall over her shoulders in a rich red cloud.

" You are much better ?"

" Thanks to you, very much ; thanks to you !" and her little hand came out frankly, and was speedily swallowed up in his big palm.

" No thanks at all; that is—well, you know. Let us change the subject. I came to say—that— that—"

" You hesitate because you are afraid of hurting my feelings. I think I can under-stand. I have learnt the world—God knows in no easy school; you came to say that I had been long enough a pensioner on your cha-rity, and now must make my own way. Isn't that it ?"

" No, indeed ; not, that is not entirely what I meant. You see—our meeting—so strange—"

" Strange enough for London and this present day. You found me starving, dying, and you took care of me ; and you knew nothing of me— not even my name—not even my appearance."

There was a something harsh and bitter in her tone which Geoffrey had never remarked before. It jarred on his ear ; but he did not further notice it. His eyes dropped a little as he said, " No, I didn't ; I do not know your name."

She looked up at him from under her eyelids ; and the harshness had all faded out of her voice as she said, " My name is Margaret Dacre." She stopped, and looked at him ; but his face only wore its grave honest smile. Then she suddenly raised - herself on the sofa, and looking straight into his face, said hurriedly, " You are a kind man, Mr. Ludlow ; a kind, generous, honourable man ; there are many men would have given me food and shelter—there are very few who would have done it unquestioning, as you have."

" You were my guest, Miss Dacre, and that

was enough, though the temptation was strong. How one evidently born and bred a lady could have—"

"Ah, now," said she, smiling faintly, "you are throwing off your bonds, and all man's curiosity is at work."

"No, on my honour; but—I don't know whether you know, but any one acquainted with the world would see that—gad! I scarcely know how to put it—but—fact is, that—people would scarcely understand—you must excuse me, but—but the position, Miss Dacre!" and Geoff pushed his hands through his hair, and knew that his cheeks were flaming.

"I see what you mean," said she, "and you are only explaining what I have for the last day or two felt myself; that the—the position must be altered. But you have so far been my friend, Mr. Ludlow—for I suppose the preserver of one's life is to be looked upon as a friend, at all events as one actuated by friendly motives—that I must ask you to advise me how to support it."

"It would be impossible to advise unless—I

mean, unless one knew, or had some idea—what, in fact, one had been accustomed to."

The girl sat up on the sofa, and this time looked him steadily in the face for a minute or so. Then she said in a calm unbroken voice, " You are coming to what I knew must arise, to what is always asked, but what I hitherto have always refused to tell. You, however, have a claim to know—what I suppose people would call my history." Her thin lips were tightly pressed and her nostrils curved in scorn as she said these words. Geoffrey marked the change, and spoke out at once, all his usual hesitation succumbing before his earnestness of purpose.

" I have asked nothing," said he; " please to remember that; and further, I wish to hear nothing. You are my guest for so long as it pleases you to remain in that position. When you wish to go, you will do so, regretted but certainly unquestioned." If Geoffrey Ludlow ever looked handsome, it was at this moment. He was a little nettled at being suspected of patronage, and the annoyance flushed his cheek and fired his eyes.

"Then I am to be a kind of heroine of a German fairy-tale; to appear, to sojourn for a while—then to fade away and never to be heard of ever after, save by the good fortune which I leave behind me to him who had entertained an angel unawares. Not the last part of the story, I fear, Mr. Ludlow; nor indeed any part of it. I have accepted your kindness; I am grateful—God knows how grateful for it—and now, being strong again—you need not raise your eyebrows; I am strong, am I not, compared with the feeble creature you found in the streets?—I will fade away, leaving gratitude and blessings behind me."

"But what do you intend to do?"

"Ah! there you probe me beyond any possibility of reply. I shall—"

"I—I have a notion, Miss Dacre, just come upon me. It was seeing you with your hair down —at least, I think it was—suggested it; but I'm sure it's a good one. To sit, you know, as a model —of course I mean your face, you know, and hair, and all that sort of thing, so much in vogue just now; and so many fellows would be delighted

to get studies of you—the pre-Raphaelite fellows,
you know; and it isn't much—the pay, you know:
but when one gets a connection—and I'm sure
that I could recommend—O, no end of fellows."
It was not that this was rather a longer speech
than usual that made Geoffrey terminate it abruptly; it was the expression in Margaret Dacre's
gray eyes.

"Do you think I could become a model, Mr.
Ludlow—at the beck and call of every man who
chose to offer me so much per hour? Would you
wish to see me thus?" and as she said the last
words she knit her brows, leaning forward and
looking straight at him under her drooping lids.

Geoffrey's eyes fell before that peculiar glance,
and he pushed his hands through his hair in sheer
doubtful desperation.

"No!" he said, after a minute's pause; "it
wouldn't do. I hadn't thought of that. You see,
I—O, by Jove, another idea! You play? Yes,
I knew you did by the look of your hands! and
talk French and German, I daresay? Ah, I
thought so! Well, you know, I give lessons in

some capital families—drawing and water-colour sketching—and I'm constantly asked if I know of governesses. Now what's to prevent my recommending you?"

"What, indeed? You have known me so long! You are so thoroughly acquainted with my capabilities—so persuaded of my respectability!"

The curved lips, the petulant nostril, the harsh bitter voice again! Geoff winced under them. "I think you are a little prejudiced," he began. "A little—"

"A little nothing! Listen, Mr. Ludlow! You have saved me from death, and you are kind enough to wish me, under your auspices, to begin life again. Hear, first, what was my former life. Hear it, and then see the soundness of your well-intentioned plans. My father was an infantry captain, who was killed in the Crimea. After the news came of his death, my mother's friends, wealthy tradespeople, raised a subscription to pay her an annuity of 150l., on condition of her never troubling them again. She accepted this, and she

and I went to live for cheapness at Tenby in
Wales. There was no break in my life until two
years since, when I was eighteen years old. Up
to that time, school, constant practice at home (for
I determined to be well educated), and attendance
on my mother, an invalid, formed my life. Then
came the usual character — without which the
drama of woman's life is incomplete—a man!"

She hesitated for a moment, and looked up as
Geoffrey Ludlow leaned forward, breathing thickly ·
through his nostrils; then she continued,—

"This one was a soldier, and claimed acquaintance with a dead comrade's widow; had his claim
allowed, and came to us morning, noon, and
night. A man of the world, they called him;
could sit and talk with my mother of her husband's virtues and still-remembered name, and
press my hand, and gaze into my eyes, and whisper in my ear whenever her head was turned."

" And you?"

" And I! What would a girl do, brought up
at a sleepy watering-place, and seeing nobody but
the curate or the doctor? I listened to his every

word, I believed his every look; and when he said to me, 'On such a night fly with me,' I fled with him without remorse."

Geoffrey Ludlow must have anticipated something of this kind, and yet when he heard it, he dropped his head and shook it, as though under the effect of a staggering blow. The action was not unnoticed by Margaret.

" Ah," said she, in low tones and with a sad smile, " I saw how your schemes would melt away before my story."

This time it was his hand that came out and caught hers in its grip.

" Ah, wait until you have heard the end, now very close at hand. The old, old story: a coming marriage, which never came, protracted and deferred now for one excuse, now for another,—the fear of friends, the waiting for promotion, the— ah, every note in the whole gamut of lies! And then—"

" Spare yourself and me—I know enough!"

" No; hear it out! It is due to you, it is due to me. A sojourn in Italy, a sojourn in England

—gradual coolness, final flight.   But such flight!
One line to say that he was ruined, and would
not drag me down in his degradation—no hope
of a future meeting—no provision for present
want.   I lived for a time by the sale of what he
had given me,—first jewels, then luxuries, then—
clothes.   And then, just as I dropped into death's
jaws, you found me."

"Thank God!" said Geoffrey earnestly, still
retaining the little hand within his own; "thank
God! I can hear no more to-day—yes; one thing,
his name?"

"His name," said she, with fixed eyes, "I
have never mentioned to mortal; but to you I will
tell it.   His name was Leonard Brookfield."

"Leonard Brookfield," repeated Geoffrey.   "I
shall not forget it.   Now adieu!   We shall meet
to-morrow."

He bowed over her hand and pressed it to his
lips, then was gone; but as his figure passed the
window, she raised herself upright, and ere he
vanished from her sight, from between her com-
pressed lips came the words, "At last! at last!"

CHAPTER IX.

WHAT is a dull life? In what does the enjoyment
of existence consist? It is a comparative matter,
after all, I fancy. A Londoner, cantering home-
ward down the Row, will lift his hat as he passes
three horsemen abreast, the middle one of whom,
comely, stout, and pleasant-looking, bows in return; or, looking after an olive-coloured brougham
with a white horse, out of the window of which
looms a lined leery-looking face, will say, " How
well Pam holds out!" and will go home to dinner
without bestowing another thought on the subject;
whereas the mere fact of having seen the Prince
of Wales or Lord Palmerston would give a coun-
tryman matter for reflection and conversation for
a couple of days. There are even Londoners who
look upon a performance of chamber-music, or a

visit to the Polytechnic Institute as an excitement;
while in a provincial town to attend a lecture on
" Mnemonics," or the dinner of the farmers' club,
is the acme of dissipation. Some lives are passed
in such a whirl that even the occasional advent
among their kindred of the great date-marker,
Death, is scarcely noticed; others dwindle away
with such unvarying pulsations that the purchase
of a new bonnet, the lameness of an old horse, the
doctor's visit, the curate's cough, are all duly set
down as notabilia worthy to be recorded. Who
does not recollect the awe and reverence with
which one regarded the Bishop of Bosphorus,
when, a benevolent seraph in a wig (they wore
wigs in those days) and lawn sleeves, he arrived
at the parish-church for the confirmation-service?
It was exciting to see him ; it was almost too much
to hear his voice ; but now, if you are a member
of the Athenæum Club, you may see him, and two
or three other prelates, reading the evening papers,
or drinking their pint of sherry with the joint, and
speaking to the waiters in voices akin to those of
ordinary mortals ; may even see him sitting next

to Belmont the poet, whose *Twilight Musings* so delighted your youth, but whom you now find to be a fat man with a red face and a tendency to growl if there be not enough schalot sent up with his steak.

If there were ever a man who should have felt the influence of a dull life, it was Lord Caterham, who never repined. And yet it would be difficult to imagine any thing more terribly lonely than was that man's existence. Dressed by his servant, his breakfast over, and he wheeled up to his library-table, there was the long day before him; how was he to get through it? Who would come to see him? His father, perhaps, for five minutes, with a talk about the leading topic treated of in the *Times*, a remark about the change in the weather, a hope that his son would " get out into the sunshine," and as speedy a departure as could be decently managed. His mother, very rarely, and then only for a frosty peck at his cheek, and a tittered hope that he was better. His brother Lionel, when in town, when not else engaged, when not too seedy after " a night of it,"—his

brother Lionel, who would throw himself into an
easy-chair, and, kicking out his slippered feet, tell
Caterham what a "rum fellow" he, Lionel, thought
him; what a "close file;" what a "reserved oys-
ter-like kind of a cove!" Other visitors occasionally. Algy Barford, genial, jolly, and quaint;
always welcome for his bright sunshiny face, his
equable temper, his odd salted remarks on men
and things. A bustling apothecary, with telescopic
shoulders and twinkling eyelids, who peered down
Lord Caterham's throat like a magpie looking into
a bone, and who listened to the wheezings of Lord
Caterham's chest with as much intentness as a
foreigner in the Opera-pit to the prayer in *Der
Freischütz*. Two or three lounging youths, fresh
from school or college, who were pleased to go
away afterwards and talk of their having been
with him, partly because he was a lord, partly
because he was a man whose name was known in
town, and one with whom it was rather *kudos* to
be thought intimate. There are people who, under
such circumstances, would have taken their servants into their confidence; but Lord Caterham

was not one of these. Kindly and courteous to all,
he yet kept his servant at the greatest distance;
and the man knew that to take the slightest liberty
was more than his place was worth. There were
no women to talk with this exile from his species;
there were none on sufficiently intimate footing to
call on him and sit with him, to talk frankly and
unreservedly that pleasant chatter which gives us
the key-note to their characters; and for this at
least Lord and Lady Beauport were unfeignedly
thankful. Lord Beauport's knowledge of the world
told him that there were women against whom his
son's deformity and isolated state would be no
defence, to whom his rank and position would be
indefinable attractions, by whom he would probably be assailed, and with whom he had no
chance of coping. Not bad women, not *intrigantes*,
—such would have set forth their charms and
wasted their dalliances in vain,—but clever heartless girls, brought up by match-making mothers,
graduates in the great school of life, skilled in the
deft and dexterous use of all aggressive weapons,
unscrupulous as to the mode of warfare so long as

victory was to be the result. In preventing Lord
Caterham from making the acquaintance of any
such persons, Lord Beauport took greater pains
than he had ever bestowed on any thing in connection with his eldest son; and, aided by the
astute generalship of his wife, he had succeeded
wonderfully.

Only once did there seem a chance of an
enemy's scaling the walls and entering the citadel,
and then the case was really serious. It was at
an Eton and Harrow match at Lord's that Lord
Caterham first saw Carry Chesterton. She came
up hanging on the arm of her brother, Con Chesterton, the gentleman farmer, who had the ground
outside Homershams, Lady Beauport's family
place, and who begged to present his sister to
Lord Caterham, of whom she had heard so much.
A sallow-faced girl, with deep black eyes, arched
brows, and raven hair in broad bands, with a
high forehead and a chiselled nose and tight
thin lips, was Carry Chesterton; and as she bent
over Lord Caterham's chair and expressed her
delight at the introduction, she shot a glance

that went through Caterham's eyes, and into his very soul.

"She was a poetess, was Carry, and all that sort of thing," said honest Con; "and had come up to town to try and get some of her writings printed, you know, and that sort of thing; and your lordship's reputation as a man of taste, you know, and that sort of thing,—if you'd only look at the stuff and give your opinion, and that sort of thing."

"That sort of thing," i.e. the compulsory conversion into a Mecænas, Lord Caterham had had tried-on before; but only in the case of moonstruck men, never from such a pair of eyes. Never had he had the request indorsed in such a deeptoned thrilling voice; and so he acquiesced, and a meeting was arranged for the morrow, when Con was to bring Carry to St. Barnabas Square; and that night Lord Caterham lay in a pleasant state of fevered excitement, thinking of his expected visitor. Carry came next day, but not Con. Con had some arrangements to make about that dreadful yeomanry which took up so much of his time, to see Major Latchford or Lord Spurrier, the colonel, and arrange about their horrid evolutions; but Carry came, and brought her manuscript book of poems. Would she read them? she could, and did, in a deep low *traînante* voice, with wonderful art and pathos, illustrating them with elevations of her thick brows and with fervid glances from her black eyes. They were above the average of women's verse, had nothing namby-pamby in them, and were not merely flowing and musical, but strong and fervid; they were full of passion, which was not merely a Byronic *refrain*, but had a warmth and novelty of its own. Lord Caterham was charmed with the verses, was charmed with the writer; he might suggest certain improvements in them, none in her. He pointed out certain lines which might be altered; and as he pointed them out, their hands met, touched but for an instant, and on looking up, his eyes lost themselves in hers.

Ah, those hand-touches and eye-glances! The oldest worldling has some pleasure in them yet, and can recall the wild ecstatic thrill which ran through him when he first experienced them in his salad-days. But we can conceive nothing of their effect on a man who, under peculiar circumstances, had lived a reserved self-contained life until five-and-twenty years of age,—a man with keen imagination and warm passions, who had "never felt the kiss of love, nor maiden's hand in his," until his whole being glowed and tingled under the fluttering touch of Carry Chesterton's lithe fingers, and in the fiery gaze of her black eyes. She came again and again; and after every visit Lord Caterham's passion increased. She was a clever woman with a purpose, to the fulfilment of which her every word, her every action, tended. Softly, delicately, and with the greatest *finesse*, she held up to him the blank dreariness of his life, and showed him how it might be cheered and consoled. In a pitying rather than an accusing spirit, she pointed out the shortcomings of his own relatives, and indicated how, to a person in his position, there could be but one who should be all in all. This was all done with the utmost tact and refinement; a sharp word, an appearance of

eagerness, the slightest showing of the cards, and
the game would have been spoilt; but Carry Chesterton knew her work, and did it well. She had
been duly presented by Lord Caterham to his
father and mother, and had duly evoked first their
suspicion, then their rage. At first it was thought
that by short resolute measures the evil might be
got rid of. So Lord Beauport spoke seriously to
his son, and Lady Beauport spoke warningly; but
all in vain. For the first time in his life Lord
Caterham rebelled, and in his rebellion spoke his
mind; and in speaking his mind he poured forth
all that bitterness of spirit which had been collect-
ing and fermenting so long. To the crippled
man's heartwrung wail of contempt and neglect,
to his passionate appeal for some one to love and
to be loved by, the parents had no reply. They
knew that he had bitter cause for complaint; but
they also knew that he was now in pursuit of a
shadow; that he was about to assuage his thirst
for love with Dead-Sea apples; that the "set gray
life and apathetic end" were better than the wild
fierce conflict and the warming of a viper in the

fires of one's heart. Lady Beauport read Carry Chesterton like a book, saw her ends and aims, and told Lord Caterham plainly what they were. " This girl is attracted by your title and position, Caterham,—nothing else," she said, in her hard dry voice ; " and the natural result has ensued." But that voice had never been softened by any infusion of maternal love. Her opinions had no weight with her son. He made no answer, and the subject dropped.

Lionel Brakespere, duly apprised by his mother of what was going on, and urged to put a stop to it, took his turn at his brother, and spoke with his usual mess-room frankness, and in his usual engaging language. " Every body knew Carry Chesterton," he said ; " all the fellows at the Rag knew her ; at least all who'd been quartered in the neighbourhood of Flockborough, where she was a regular garrison hack, and had been engaged to Spoonbill of the 18th Hussars, and jilted by Slummer of the 160 Rifles, and was as well known as the town-clock, by Jove ; and Caterham was a flat and a spoon, and he'd be

dashed if he'd see the fam'ly degraded; and I
say, why the doose didn't Caterham listen to
reason!"   So far Captain the Honourable Lionel
Brakespere; who, utterly failing in his purpose
and intent, and having any further access to Lord
Caterham's rooms strictly denied him by Lord
Caterham's orders, sought out Algy Barford and
confided to him the whole story, and "put him
on" to save the fam'ly credit, and stop Caterham's
rediklous 'fatuation.

Now if the infatuation in question had been
legitimate, and likely to lead to good results, Algy
Barford would have been the very last man on
earth to attempt to put a stop to it, or to interfere
in any way save for its advancement.   But this
airy, laughing philosopher, with all his apparent
carelessness, was a man of the world and a shrewd
reader of human character; and he had made
certain inquiries, the result of which proved that
Carry Chesterton was, if not all that Lionel Break-
spere had made her out, at all events a heartless
coquette and fortune-huntress, always rising at
the largest fly.   Quite recently jilted by that

charming creature Captain Slummer of the Rifles, she had been heard to declare she would not merely retrieve the position hereby lost, but achieve a much greater one; and she had been weak enough to boast of her influence over Lord Caterham, and her determination to marry him in spite of all his family's opposition. Then Algy Barford joined the ranks of the conspirators, and brought his thoroughly practical worldly knowledge to their camp. It was at a council held in Lady Beauport's boudoir that he first spoke on the subject, his face radiant with good humour, his teeth gleaming in the light, and his attention impartially divided between the matter under discussion and the vagaries of a big rough terrier which accompanied him every where.

"You must pardon me, dear Lady Beauport," said he; "but you've all been harking forward on the wrong scent.—Down, Tinker! Don't let him jump on your mother, Lionel; his fleas, give you my honour, big as lobsters!—on the wrong scent! Dear old Caterham, best fellow in the world; but frets at the curb, don't you know?

Put him a couple of links higher up than usual, and he rides rusty and jibs—jibs, by Jove! And that's what you've been doing now. Dear old Caterham! not much to amuse him in life, don't you know? goes on like a blessed old martyr; but at last finds something which he likes, and you don't. Quite right, dear Lady Beauport; *I* see it fast enough, because I'm an old lad, and have seen men and cities; but dear Caterham, who is all milk and rusks and green peas, and every thing that is innocent, don't you know, don't see it at all. And then you try to shake him by the shoulder and rouse him out of his dream, and tell him that he's not in fairyland, not in Aladdin's palace, not in a two-pair back in Craven Street, Strand. Great mistake that, Lionel, dear boy. Dear Lady Beauport, surely your experience teaches you that it is a great mistake to cross a person when they're in that state?"

"But, Mr. Barford, what is to be done?"

"Put the helm about, Lady Beauport, and— Tinker! you atrocious desperado, you shameless caitiff! will you get down?—put the helm about, and try the other tack. We've failed with dear old Caterham: now let's try the lady. Caterham is the biggest fish she's seen yet; but my notion is that if a perch came in her way, and seemed likely to bite, she'd forget she'd ever seen a gudgeon. Now my brother Windermere came to town last week, and he's an earl, you know, and just the sort of fellow who likes nothing so much as a flirtation, and is all the time thunderingly well able to take care of himself. I think if Miss Chesterton were introduced to Windermere, she'd soon drop poor dear Caterham."

Both Lionel and his mother agreed in this notion, and an early opportunity was taken for the presentation of Lord Windermere to Miss Chesterton. An acknowledged *parti;* a man of thews and sinews; frank, generous, and affable: apparently candid and unsuspecting in the highest degree, he seemed the very prize for which that accomplished fortune-huntress had long been waiting; and forgetting the old fable of the shadow and the substance, she at once turned a decided cold shoulder upon poor Lord Caterham, ceased

visiting him, showed him no more poetry, and
within a week of her making Lord Windermere's acquaintance, cut her old friend dead in
Kensington Gardens, whither he had been wheeled
in the hope of seeing her. Ah, in how few weeks,
having discovered the sandy foundation on which
she had been building, did she come back, crouch-
ing and fawning and trying all the old devices,
to find the fire faded out of Caterham's eyes and
the hope out of his breast, and the prospect of
any love or companionship as distant from him
as ever!

Yes, that was Lord Caterham's one experience
of love; and after its lame and impotent conclusion he determined he would never have another.
We have all of us determined that in our time;
but few of us have kept to our resolution so rigidly
as did Lord Caterham, possibly because opportu-
nities have not been so wanting to us as to him.
It is all that horrible opportunity which saps our
strongest resolutions; it is the close proximity of
the magnum of "something special" in claret
which leads to the big drink; it is the shaded

walk, and the setting sun behind the deep bank
of purple clouds, and the solemn stillness, and
the upturned eyes and the provoking mouth,
which lead to all sorts of horrible mistakes. Opportunity after the Chesterton *escapade* was denied
to Lord Caterham both by himself and his parents. He shut himself up in solitude : he would
see no one save the apothecary and Algy Barford, who indeed came constantly, feeling all the
while horribly treacherous and shamefaced. And
then by degrees—by that blessed process of Time
against which we rail so much, but which is so
beneficial, of Time the anodyne and comforter,
he fell back into his old ways of life ; and all that
little storm and commotion was as though it had
never been. It left no marks of its fury on Caterham ; he kept no relics of its bright burning
days : all letters had been destroyed. There was
not a glove nor a flower in his drawers—nothing
for him to muse and shake his head over. So
soon as his passion had spent itself—so soon as
he could look calmly upon the doings of the
few previous months, he saw how unworthy they

had been, and blotted them from his memory for ever.

So until Annie Maurice had come to take up her position as his mother's companion, Lord Caterham had been entirely without female society, and since her advent he had first learned the advantages of associating with a pure, genuine healthy woman. Like Carry Chesterton, she seemed to take to the crippled man from her first introduction to him ; but ah, how unlike that siren did sweet Annie Maurice show her regard ! There was no more romance in her composition, so she would have told you herself, than in the statue at Charing Cross ; no eyebrow elevations, no glances, no palpable demonstrations of interest. In quite a household and domestic manner did this good fairy discharge her duties. She was not the Elf, the Wili, the Giselle, in book-muslin and starsprent hair; she was the ordinary " Brownie," the honest Troll, which shows its presence in help rather than ornament. Ever since Miss Maurice had been an inmate of the house in Barnabas Square, Caterham's books had been dusted, his books and papers arranged, his diurnal calendar set, his desk freshened with a glass of newly-gathered flowers. Never before had his personal wants been so readily understood, so deftly attended to. No one smoothed his pillows so softly, wheeled his chair so easily, his every look so quickly comprehended. To all that dreary household Annie Maurice was a sunbeam ; but on no one did she shine so brightly as on that darkened spirit. The Earl felt the beaming influence of her bright nature ; the Countess could not deny her meed of respect to one who was always " in her place ;" the servants, horribly tenacious of interference, could find no fault with Miss Maurice ; but to none appeared she in so bright a light as to Lord Caterham.

It was the morning after the receipt of the letter which Algy Barford had left with him, and which had seemingly so much upset him, that Caterham was sitting in his room, his hands clasped idly before him, his looks bent, not on the book lying open on the desk, but on the vacant space beyond it. So delicately constituted was his

frame, that any mental jar was immediately succeeded by acute bodily suffering; he was hurt,
not merely in spirit but in body; the machinery of
his being was shaken and put out of gear, and
it took comparatively some length of time for all
to get into working order again. The strain on
this occasion had evidently been great, his head
throbbed, his eyes were surrounded with bistre
rings, and the nervous tension of his clasped
fingers showed the unrest of his mind. Then
came a gentle tap on the door, a sound apparently
instantly recognisable, for Lord Caterham raised
his head, and bade the visitor "Come in." It was
Annie Maurice. No one else opened the door so
quickly and closed it so quietly behind her, no one
came with so light and yet so firm a step, no one
else would have seen that the sun was pouring in
through the window on to the desk, and would
have crossed the room and arranged the blind
before coming up to the chair. Caterham knew
her without raising his eyes, and had said, "Ah,
Annie dear!" before she reached him.

"I feared you were ill, my lord," she commenced; but a deep growl from Caterham stopped her. " I feared you were ill, Arthur," she then said ; " you did not show at dinner last night, nor in the evening ; but I thought you might be disinclined for society—the Gervises were here, you know, and the Scrimgeours, and I know you don't care for our classical music, which is invariable on such occasions ; but I met Stephens on the staircase, and he gave me such a desponding account, that I really feared you were ill."

" Only a passing dull fit, Annie ; only a passing dull fit of extra heaviness, and consequently extra duration !   Stephens is a croaker, you know ; and having, I believe, an odd sort of Newfoundland-dog, attachment to me, is frightened if I have a finger-ache.   But I'm very glad you've come in, Annie, for I'm not really very bright even now, and you always help to set me straight.   Well, and how goes it with you, young lady ?"

" Oh, very well, Arthur, very well."

" You feel happier than you did on your first coming among us ?   You feel as though you were settling down into your home ?"

"I should be worse than foolish if I did not, for every one tries to be kind to me."

"I did not ask you for moral sentiments, Annie, I asked you for facts. Do you feel settling down into your home?" And as Caterham said this, he shot a keen scrutinising glance at the girl.

She paused for a moment ere she answered, and when she spoke she looked at him straight out of her big brown eyes.

"Do I feel as if I were settling down into my home, Arthur? No; in all honesty, no. I have no home, as you know well enough; but I feel that—"

"Why no home?" he interrupted; "isn't—No, I understand."

"No, you do not understand; and it is for that reason I speak. You do not understand me, Lord—Arthur. You have notions which I want to combat, and set right at once, please. I know you have, for I've heard hints of them in something you've said before. It all rises out of your gentlemanly and chivalrous feeling, I know; but, believe me, you're wrong. I fill the position of your mother's companion here, and you have fallen into the conventional notion that I'm not well treated, put upon, and all that kind of thing. On my honour, that is utterly wrong. No two people could be kinder, after their lights, than Lord and Lady Beauport are to me. Of your own conduct I need say no word. From the servants I have perfect respect; and yet—"

"And yet?"

"Well, simply you chose the wrong word; there's no homey feeling about it, and I should be false were I to pretend there were."

"But pardon me for thus pursuing the subject into detail,—my interest in you must be my excuse,—what 'homey feeling,' as you call it, had you at Ricksborough Vicarage, whence you came to us? The people there are no closer blood-relations than we are; nor did they, as far as I know—"

"Nor did they try more to make me happy. No, indeed, they could not have tried more in that way than you do. But I was much younger

when I first went there, Arthur—quite a little
child—and had all sorts of childish reminiscences
of cow-milking, and haymaking, and harvest-
homes, and all kinds of ruralities, with that great
balloon-shaped shadow of St. Paul's ever present on the horizon keeping watch over the
City, where dear old uncle Frank told me I
should have to get my living after he was gone.
Its home-influence gained on me even from the
sorrow which I saw and partook of in it; from
the sight of my aunt's death-bed and my uncle's
meek resignation overcoming his desperate grief;
from the holy comfort inspired in him by the
discharge of his holy calling; by the respect
and esteem in which he was held by all around,
and which was never so much shown as when
he wanted it most acutely. These things, among
many others, made that place home to me."

"Yes," said Lord Caterham, in a harsh dry
voice; "I understand easily enough. After such
innocence and goodness I can fully comprehend what it must be to you to read blue-
books to my father, to listen to my mother's

fade nonsense about balls, operas, and dresses, or to attend to the hypochondriacal fancies of a valetudinarian like myself—"

" Lord Caterham! I don't think that even you have a right to insult me in this way!"

" *Even* I! thank you for the compliment, which implies—Bah! what a brute I am! You'll forgive me, Annie, won't you? I'm horribly hipped and low. I've not been out for two days; and the mere fact of being a prisoner to the house always fills my veins with bile instead of blood. Ah, you won't keep that knit brow and those tightened lips any longer, will you? No one sees more plainly than I do that your life here wants certain—"

" Pray say no more, I—"

" Ah, Annie, for Heaven's sake don't pursue this miserable growl of mine. Have some pity for my ill-health. But I want to see you with as many surroundings natural to your age and taste as we can find in this—hospital. There's music: you play and sing very sweetly; but you can't—I know you can't—sit down with any

case or comfort to that great furniture-van of
a grand-piano in that gaunt drawing-room;
that's only fit for those long-haired foreigners
who let off their fire-works on Lady Beauport's
reception-nights. You must have a good piano
of your own, in your own room or here, or
somewhere where you can practise quietly. I'll
see about that. And drawing—for you have a
great natural talent for that; but you should
have some lessons: you must keep it up; you
must have a master. There's a man goes to
Lady Lilford's, a capital fellow, whom I know;
you must have him. What's his name? Ludlow—"

"What, Geoffrey Ludlow! dear old Geoff!
He used to be papa's greatest friend when we
were at Willesden, you know,—and before that
dreadful bankruptcy, you know, Mr. Ludlow
was always there. I've sat on his knee a thousand times; and he used to sketch me, and call
me his little elf. Oh yes, dear Arthur, I should
like that,—I should like to have lessons from Mr.
Ludlow! I should so like to see him again!"

" Well, Annie, you shall. I'll get his address from the Lilfords and write to him, and settle about his coming. And now, Annie, leave me, dear; I'm a little tired, and want rest."

He was tired, and wanted rest; but he did not get it just then. Long after Annie left the room he sat pondering, pondering, with a strange feeling for which he himself could not account, but which had its key-note in this: How strongly she spoke of the man Ludlow; how he disliked her earnestness on the subject; and what would he not have given, could he have thought she would have spoken so strongly of him.

CHAPTER X.

WHEN you feel yourself gradually becoming en-
thralled, falling a victim to a fascination all-
potent, but scarcely all-satisfactory, be it melancholy, or gambling, or drink, or love, there is
nothing so counteracting to the horrible influence
as to brace your nerves together, and go in for
a grand spell of work. That remedy is always
efficacious, of course. It never fails, as Geoffrey
Ludlow knew very well; and that was the reason why, on the morning after his last described
interview with Margaret Dacre, he dragged out
from behind a screen, where it had been turned
with its face to the wall, his half-finished picture intended for the Academy, and commenced
working on it with wonderful earnestness. It
was a large canvas with three principal figures:

a young man, a "swell" of modern days, turning away from the bold and eager glances of a
somewhat brazen coquette, and suddenly struck
by the modest bashful beauty of a girl of the
governess-order seated at a piano. "Scylla and
Charybdis" Geoff had intended calling it, with
the usual *Incidit in* &c. motto; and when the
idea first struck him he had taken pains with
his composition, had sketched his figures carefully, and had painted-in the flirt and the man
very successfully. The governess had as yet
been a failure; he had had no ideal to work
from; the model who had sat to him was a
little coarse and clumsy, and irritated at not
being able to carry out his notion, he had put
the picture by. But he now felt that work was
required of him, not merely as a distraction
from thought, but as an absolute duty which he
owed to himself; and as this was a subject
likely to be appreciated by Mr. Stompff, he determined to work at it again, and to have it
ready for submission to the Hanging Committee
of the Academy. He boggled over it a little

at first; he smoked two pipes, staring at the
canvas, occasionally shading his eyes with one
hand, and waving the other in a dreamy pos-
sessed manner in front of him. Then he took
up a brush and began to lay on a bit of colour,
stepping back from time to time to note the
effect; and then the spirit came upon him, and
he went to work with all his soul.

What a gift is that of the painter, whose whole
story can be read at one glance, who puts what
we require three thick volumes to narrate into a
few feet of canvas, who with one touch of his
brush gives an expression which we pin-and-ink
workers should take pages to convey, and even
then could never hope to do it half so happily!—
who sees his work grow beneath his hand, and
can himself judge of its effect on others;—who
can sit with his pipe in his mouth, and chirp away
merrily to his friend, the while his right hand is
gaining him wealth and honour and fame!

The spirit was on Geoffrey Ludlow, and the
result came out splendidly. He hoped to gain
a good place on the Academy walls, he hoped to

do justice to the commissions which Mr. Stompff had given him; but there was something beyond these two incentives which spurred his industry and nerved his touch. After all his previous failures, it seemed as though Scylla the governess would have the best of it at last. Charybdis was a splendid creature, a bold, black-eyed, raven-haired charmer, with her hair falling in thick masses over her shoulders, and with a gorgeous passion-flower hanging voluptuously among her tresses; a goddess amongst big Guardsmen, who would sit and suck their yellow moustaches and express their admiration in fragmentary ejaculations, or amongst youths from the Universities, with fluff instead of hair, and blushes in place of *aplomb*. But in his later work the artist's heart seemed to have gone with Scylla, who was to her rival as is a proof after Sir Joshua to a French print, as a glass of Amontillado to a *petit verre* of Chartreuse,— a slight delicate creature, with violet eyes and pallid complexion, and deep-red hair brought down in thick braids, and tucked away behind such dainty little ears; her modest

gray dress contrasting, in its quaker-like simplicity, with the brilliant-hued robe and rich laces
of her rival.   His morning's work must have
been successful; for—rare thing with him—Geoff
himself was pleased with it; no doubt of the
inspiration now, he tried to deny it to himself,
but could not—the likeness came out so wonderfully.   So he gave way to the charm, and as he
sat before the canvas, thoughtfully gazing at it, he
let his imagination run riot, and gave his pleasant
memories full play.

He had worked well and manfully, and had
tolerably satisfied himself, and was sitting resting,
looking at what he had done, and thinking over
what had prompted his work, when there came
a tap at the door, and his sister Til crept noiselessly in.   She entered softly, as was her wont
when her brother was engaged, and took up her
position behind him.   But Miss Til was demon-
strative by nature, and after a minute's glance
could not contain herself.

"Oh, you dear old Geoff, that is charming;
oh, Geoff, how you have got on!   But I say,

Geoff, the governess—what do you call her? I never can recollect those Latin names, or Greek is it?—you know, and it does not matter; but she is—you know, Geoff, I know you don't like me to say so, but I can't find any other word— she is stunning! Not that I think—I don't know, you know, of course, because we don't mix in that sort of society—not that—that I think that people who—well, I declare, I don't know any other word for them!—I mean swells—would allow their governess to have her hair done in that style; but she is de-licious! You've got a new model, Geoff; at least you've never attempted any thing in that style before, and I declare you've made a regular hit. You don't speak, Geoff; don't you like what I'm saying?"

"My dear child, you don't give me the chance of saying any thing. You rattle on with 'I know' and 'you know' and 'don't you know,' till I can scarcely tell where I am. One thing I do manage to glean, however, and that is that you are pleased with the picture, which is the very best news that I could have. For though you're a most horrible little rattletrap, and talk nineteen to the dozen, there is some sense in what you say and always a great deal of truth."

" Specially when what I say is complimentary, eh, Geoff? Not that I think I have ever said much in any other strain to you. But you haven't told me about your new model, Geoff. Where did she come from ?"

" My new model?"

" Yes, yes, for the governess, you know. That's new — I mean that hair and eyes, and all that. You've never painted any thing like that before. Where did she come from ?"

There were few things that Geoffrey Ludlow would have kept from his sister, but this was one of them ; so he merely said :

" O, a model, Til dear — one of the usual shilling-an-hour victims."

" Sent you by Mr. Charles Potts, I suppose," said Miss Til, with unusual asperity; " sent you for—" But here a knock at the door cut short the young lady's remarks. " O, but if that is Mr. Potts," she resumed, " don't say a word about what I said just now; don't, Geoff, there's a dear."

It was not Mr. Potts who responded to Geoffrey Ludlow's "Come in." It was Mr. Bowker's head which was thrust through the small space made by the opening of the door; and it was Mr. Bowker's deep voice which exclaimed:

"Engaged, eh? Your William will look in again."

But Til, with whom Mr. Bowker was a special favourite, from his strange unconventional manners and rough *bonhomie*, called out at once: "Mr. Bowker, it's only I—Geoff's sister Til;" and Geoff himself roaring out that "Bowker was growing modest in his old age," that gentleman was persuaded to come in; and closing the door lightly behind him, he went up to the young lady, and bending over her hand, made her a bow such as any *preux chevalier* might have envied. A meeting with a lady was a rare oasis in the desert of William Bowker's wasted life; but whenever he had the chance he showed that he had been something more than the mere pot-walloping boon-companion which most men thought him.

"Geoff's sister Til!" he repeated, looking at the tall handsome girl before him,—"Geoff's sister Til! Ah, then it's perfectly right that I should have lost all my hair, and that my beard should be grizzled, and that I have a general notion of the omnipresence of old age. I was inclined to grumble; but if 'Geoff's sister Til,' who I thought was still a little child, is to come up and greet me in this guise, I recant: Time is right; and your William is the only old fool in the matter."

"It is your own fault, Mr. Bowker, that you don't know the changes that take place in us. You know we are always glad to see you, and that mamma is always sending you messages by Geoff."

"You are all very good, and—well, I suppose it is my fault; let's say it is at all events. What! going? There you see the effect my presence has when I come up on a chance visit."

"Not at all," said Til; "I should have gone

five minutes ago it you had not come in. I'll make a confidant of you, Mr. Bowker, and let you into a secret. Those perpetual irritable pulls at the bell are the tradespeople waiting for orders; and I must go and settle about dinner and all sorts of things. Now good-bye." She shook hands with him, nodded brightly at her brother, and was gone.

"That's a nice girl," said William Bowker, as the door closed after her; "a regular nice girl— modest, ladylike, and true; none of your infernal fal-lal affectations—honest as the day; you can see that in her eyes and in every word she says. Where do you keep your tobacco? All right. Your pipes want looking after, Geoff. I've tried three, and each is as foul as a chimney. Ah, this will do at last; now I'm all right, and can look at your work. H—m! that seems good stuff. You must tone-down that background a little, and put a touch of light here and there on the dress, which is infernally heavy and Hamlet-like. Hallo, Geoff, are you going in for the P.-R.-B. business?"

" Not I. What do you mean?"

" What do *you* mean by this red-haired party, my boy? This is a new style for you, Geoff, and one which no one would have thought of your taking up. You weren't brought up to consider this the right style of thing in old Sassoon's academy, Geoff. If the old boy could rise from his grave, and see his favourite pupil painting a frizzy, red-haired, sallow-faced woman as the realisation of beauty, I think he'd be glad he'd been called away before such awful times."

There was a hesitation in Geoff's voice, and a hollowness in his smile, as he answered:

" P.-R.-B. nonsense! Old Sassoon couldn't teach every thing; and as for his ideas of beauty, look how often he made us paint Mrs. S. and the Miss S.'s, who, Heaven knows, were any thing but reproductions of the Venus Calipyge. The simple question, as I take it, is this — is the thing a good thing or a bad one? Tell me that."

" As a work of art?"

" Of course; as you see it. What else could I mean?"

" As a work of art, it's good—undeniably good, in tone, and treatment, and conception; as a work of prudence, it's infernally bad."

Geoff looked at him sharply for a minute, and William Bowker, calmly puffing at his pipe, did not shrink from his friend's glance. Then, with a flush, Geoff said :

" It strikes me that it is as a work of art you have to regard it. As to what you say about a work of prudence, you have the advantage of me. I don't understand you."

" Don't you?" said William. " I'm sorry for you. What model did you paint that head from ?"

" From no model."

" From life ?"

" N-no; from memory—from— Upon my soul, Bowker, I don't see what right you have to cross-question me in this way."

" Don't you?" said Bowker. " Give your William something to drink, please ; he can't

talk when he's dry. What is that? B. and soda.
Yes, that'll do. Look here, Geoffrey Ludlow,
when you were little more than a boy, grinding
away in the Life-School, and only too pleased if
the Visitor gave you an encouraging word, your
William, who is ten years your senior, had done
work which made him be looked upon as the
coming man. He had the ball at his foot, and
he had merely to kick it to send it where he
chose. He does not say this out of brag—you
know it?"

Geoffrey Ludlow inclined his head in acquiescence.

"Your William didn't kick the ball; something interfered just as his foot was lifted to
send it flying to the goal—a woman."

Again Geoffrey Ludlow nodded in acquiescence.

"You've heard the story. Every body in
town knew it, and each had his peculiar version;
but I will tell you the whole truth myself. You
don't know how I struggled on against that infatuation;—no, you may think you do, but I am
a much stronger man than you—am, or was—

and I saw what I was losing by giving way. I gave way. I knocked down the whole fabric which, from the time I had had a man's thoughts, a man's mind, a man's energy and power, I had striven to raise. I kicked it all down, as Alnaschar did his basket of eggs, and almost as soon found how vain had been my castle-building. I need scarcely go into detail with you about that story: it was published in the Sunday newspapers of the time; it echoed in every club-room; it has remained lingering about art-circles, and in them is doubtless told with great gusto at the present day, should ever my name be mentioned. I fell in love with a woman who was married to a man of more than double her age,—a woman of educa-tion, taste, and refinement; of singular beauty too —and that to a young artist was not her least charm—tied for life to an old heartless scoundrel. My passion for her sprung from the day of my first seeing her; but I choked it down. 1 saw as plainly as I see this glass before me now what would be the consequence of any absurd escapade on my part; how it would crush me, how, infi-

nitely more, it would drag *her* down. I knew
what was working in each of us; and, so help me
Heaven! I tried to spare us both. I tried—and
failed, dismally enough. It was for no want of
arguing with myself—from no want of forethought
of all the consequences that might ensue. I looked
at all point-blank; for though I was young and
mad with passion, I loved that woman so that I
could even have crushed my own selfishness lest
it should be harm to her. I could have done this:
I did it until—until one night I saw a blue livid
mark on her shoulder. God knows how many
years that is ago, but I have the whole scene before me at this moment. It was at some fine ball
(I went into what is called 'society' then), and
we were standing in a conservatory, when I noticed
this mark. I asked her about it, and she hesitated;
I taxed her with the truth, which she first feebly
denied, then admitted. He had struck her, the
hound! in a fit of jealous rage,—had struck her
with his clenched fist! Even as she told me this,
I could see him within a few yards of us, pre-
tending to be rapt in conversation, but obviously

noting our conduct. I suppose he guessed that
she had told me of what had occurred. I suppose
he guessed it from my manner and the expression
of my face, for a deadly pallor came over his
grinning cheeks; and as we passed out of the
conservatory, he whispered to her—not so low but
that I caught the words—' You shall pay for this,
madam—you shall pay for this!' That determined
me, and that night we fled.—Give me some more
brandy and soda, Geoff. Merely to tell this story
drags the heart out of my breast."

Geoff pushed the bottle over to his friend, and
after a gulp Bowker proceeded :

" We went to Spain, and remained there many
months; and there it was all very well. That
slumbering country is even now but little haunted
by your infernal British tourist; but then scarcely
any Englishman came there. Such as we came
across were all bachelors, your fine lady can't
stand the mule-travelling and the roughing it in
the posadas; and they either had not heard the
story, or didn't see the propriety of standing on
any squeamishness, more especially when the ac-

quaintance was all to their advantage, and we got
on capitally. Nelly had seen nothing, poor child,
having left school to be married; and all the travel,
and the picturesque old towns, and the peasantry,
and the Alhambra, and all the rest of it, made a
sort of romantic dream for her. But then old Van
den Bosch got his divorce; and so soon as I had
heard of that, like a madman as I was, I determined to come back to England. The money
was running short, to be sure; but I had made
no end of sketches, and I might have sent them
over and sold them; but I wanted to get back.
A man can't live on love alone; and I wanted to
be amongst my old set again, for the old gossip
and the old *camaraderie;* and so back we came.
I took a little place out at Ealing, and then I went
into the old haunts, and saw the old fellows, and
—for the first time—so help me Heaven! for the
first time I saw what I had done. They cut me,
sir, right and left! There were some of them—
blackguards who would have hobnobbed with
Greenacre, if he'd stood the drink—who accepted
my invitations, and came Sunday after Sunday,

and would have eaten and drunk me out of house
and home, if I'd have stood it; but the best—
the fellows I really cared about—pretty generally
gave me the cold shoulder. Some of them had
married during my absence, and of course they
couldn't come; others were making their way in
their art, working under the patronage of big
swells in the Academy, and hoping for election
there, and they daren't be mixed up with such a
notoriously black sheep as your William. I felt
this, Geoff, old boy. By George, it cut me to the
heart; it took all the change out of me; it made
me low and hipped, and, I fear, sometimes savage.
And I suppose I showed it at home ; for poor Nell
seemed to change and wither from the day of our
return. She had her own troubles, poor darling,
though she thought she kept them to herself.
In a case like that, Geoff, the women get it much
hotter than we do. There were no friends for her,
no one to whom she could tell her troubles. And
then the story got known, and people used to stare
and nudge each other, and whisper as she passed.
The parson called when we first came, and was a

good pleasant fellow; but a fortnight afterwards he'd heard all about it, and grew purple in the face as he looked straight over our heads when we met him. And once a butcher, who had to be spoken to for cheating, cheeked her and alluded to her story; but I think what I did to him prevented any repetition of that kind of conduct. But I couldn't silence the whole world by thrashing it, old fellow; and Nell drooped and withered under all the misery—drooped and—died! And I—well, I became the graceless, purposeless, spiritless brute you see me now!"

Mr. Bowker stopped and rubbed the back of his hand across his eyes, and gave a great cough before finishing his drink ; and then Geoffrey patted him on the shoulder and said, " But you know how we all love you, old friend; how that Charley Potts, and I, and Markham, and Wallis, and all the fellows, would do any thing for you."

Mr. Bowker gave his friend's hand a tight grip as he said, " I know, Geoff; I know you boys are fond of your William ; but it wasn't to parade my grief, or to cadge for sympathy from them, that I told you that story. I had another motive."

" And that was—"

" To set myself up as an example and a warning to—any one who might be going to take a similar step. You named yourself just now, Geoff, amongst those who cared for me. Your William is a bit of a fogy, he knows; but some of you do care for him, and you amongst them."

" Of course. You know that well enough."

" Then why not show your regard for your William, dear boy ?"

" Show my regard—how shall I show it ?"

" By confiding in him, Geoff; by talking to him about yourself; telling him your hopes and plans; asking him for some of that advice which seeing a great many men and cities, and being a remarkably downy old skittle, qualifies him to give. Why not confide in him, Geoff?"

" Confide in you? About what? Why on earth not speak out plainly at once ?"

" Well, well, I won't beat about the bush any

longer. I daresay there's nothing in it; but people talk and cackle so confoundedly, and, by George, men—some men, at least—are quite as bad as women in that line; and they say you're in love, Geoff; regularly hard hit—no chance of recovery!"

"Do they?" said Geoff, flushing very red—"do they? Who are 'they,' by the way?—not that it matters, a pack of gabbling fools! But suppose I am—what then?"

"What then! Why, nothing then—only it's rather odd that you've never told your William, whom you've known so long and so intimately, any thing about it. Is that" (pointing to the picture) "a portrait of the lady?"

"There—there is a reminiscence of her—her head and general style."

"Then your William would think that her head and general style must be doosid good. Any sisters?"

"I—I think not."

"Are her people pleasant—do you get on with them?"

"I don't know them."

"Ah, Geoff, Geoff, why make me go on in this way? Don't you know me well enough to be certain that I'm not asking all these questions for impertinence and idle curiosity? Don't you see that I'm dragging bit by bit out of you because I'm coming to the only point any of your friends can care about? Is this girl a good girl; is she respectable; is she in your own sphere of life; can you bring her home and tell the old lady to throw her arms round her neck, and welcome her as a daughter? Can you introduce her to that sweet sister of yours who was here when I came in?"

There came over Geoffrey Ludlow's face a dark shadow such as William Bowker had never seen there before. He did not speak nor turn his eyes, but sat fixed and rigid as a statue.

"For God's sake think of all this, Geoff! I've told you a thousand times that you ought to be married; that there was no man more calculated to make a woman happy, or to have his own happiness increased by a woman's love. But then she must be of your own degree in life, and one of whom you could be every where proud. I would not have you married to an ugly woman or a drabby woman, or any thing that wasn't very nice; how much less, then, to any one whom you would feel ashamed of, or who could not be received by your dear ones at home! Geoff, dear old Geoff, for heaven's sake think of all this before it is too late! Take warning by my fatal error, and see what misery you would prepare for both of you."

Geoffrey Ludlow still sat in the same attitude. He made no reply for some minutes; then he said, dreamily, "Yes—yes, you're quite right, of course, — quite right. But I don't think we'll continue the conversation now. Another time, Bowker, please—another time." Then he ceased, and Mr. Bowker rose and pressed his hand, and took his departure. As he closed the door behind him, that worthy said to himself: " Well, I've done my duty, and I know I've done right; but it's very little of Geoff's mutton that your William will cut, and very little of Geoff's wine that your

William will drink, if that marriage comes off. For of course he'll tell her all I've said, and *won't* she love your William!"

And for hours Geoffrey Ludlow sat before his easel, gazing at the Scylla head, and revolving all the detail of Mr. Bowker's story in his mind.

CHAPTER XI.

WHEN did the giver of good, sound, unpalatable, wholesome advice ever receive his due? Who does not possess, amongst the multitude of acquaintances, a friend who says, " Such and such are my difficulties: I come to you because I want advice;" and who, after having heard all that, after a long struggle with yourself, you bring yourself to say, wrings your hand, goes away thinking what an impertinent idiot you are, and does exactly the opposite of all you have suggested? All men, even the most self-opinionated and practical, are eager for advice. None, even the most hesitating and diffident, take it, unless it agrees with their own preconceived ideas. There are, of course, exceptions by which this rule is proved; but there are two subjects on which no man was ever yet known to take advice, and they are horses and women. Depreciate your friend's purchase as delicately as Agag came unto Saul; give every possible encomium to make and shape and breeding; but hint, *per contra*, that the animal is scarcely up to his weight, or that that cramped action looks like a possible blunder; suggest that a little more slope in the shoulder, a little less cowiness in the general build, might be desirable for riding purposes, and your friend will smile, and shake his head, and canter away, convinced of the utter shallowness of your equine knowledge. In the other matter it is much worse. You must be very much indeed a man's friend if you can venture to hint to him, even after his iterated requests for your honest candid opinion, that the lady of his love is any thing but what he thinks her. And though you iterate and reiterate, moralise as shrewdly as Ecclesiasticus, bring chapter and verse to support your text, he must be more or less than a man, and cast in very different clay from that of which we poor ordinary mortals are composed, if he accepts one of your argu-

ments or gives way one atom before your elucida-
tions.

Did William Bowker's forlorn story, com-
mingled with his earnest passionate appeal, weigh
one scruple with Geoffrey Ludlow? Not one.
Geoff was taken aback by the story. There was
a grand human interest in that laying bare before
him of a man's heart, and of two persons' wasted
lives, which aroused his interest and his sympathy,
made him ponder over what might have been,
had the principal actors in the drama been kept
asunder, and sent him into a fine drowsy state
of metaphysical dubiety. But while Bowker was
pointing his moral, Geoff was merely turning
over the various salient points which had adorned
his tale.

He certainly heard Bowker drawing a parallel
between his own unhappy passion and Geoff's
regard for the original owner of that "Scylla
head;" but as the eminent speaker was arguing
on hypothetical facts, and drawing deductions from
things of which he knew absolutely nothing, too
much reliance was not to be placed on his argu-

ments. In Bowker's case there had been a public scandal, a certain betrayal of trust, which was the worst feature in the whole affair, a trial and an *exposé*, and a denunciation of the—well, the world used hard words—the seducer; which—though Bowker was the best fellow in the world, and had obviously a dreadful time of it—which was only according to English custom. Now, in his own case, Margaret (he had already accustomed himself to think of her as Margaret) had been victimised by a scoundrel, and the blame—for he supposed blame would, at least in the minds of very strait-laced people, attach to her—was mitigated by the facts. Besides—and here was his great thought—nothing would be known of her former history. Her life, so far as any one in his set could possibly know any thing about it, began on the night when he and Charley Potts found her in the street. She was destitute and starving, granted; but there was nothing criminal in destitution and starvation, which indeed would, in the eyes of a great many weak and good-natured (the terms are synonymous) persons, bind a kind of romance to the story. And as to all that had gone before, what of that? How was any thing of that love ever to become known? This Leonard Brookfield, an army swell, a man who, under any circumstances, was never likely to come across them, or to be mixed up in Geoff's artist-circle, had vanished, and with him vanished the whole dark part of the story. Vanished for ever and aye! Margaret's life would begin to date from the time when she became his wife, when he brought her home to——Ah, by the way, what was that Bowker said about her worthiness to associate with his mother and sister? Why not? He would tell them all about it. They were good women, who fully appreciated the grand doctrine of forgiveness; and yet — He hesitated; he knew his mother to be a most excellent church-going woman, bearing her "cross" womanfully, not to say rather flaunting it than otherwise; but he doubted whether she would appreciate an introduction to a Magdalen, however penitent. To subscribe to a charity for "those poor creatures;" to talk pleasantly and

condescendingly to them, and to leave them a
tract on visiting a " Home" or a " Refuge," is one
thing; to take them to your heart as daughters-
in-law is another. And his sister! Well, young
girls didn't understand this kind of thing, and
would put a false construction on it, and were
always chattering, and a great deal of harm might
be done by Til's want of reticence; and so, perhaps, the best thing to be done was to hold his
tongue, decline to answer any questions about
former life, and leave matters to take their course.
He had already arrived at that state of mind that
he felt, if any disagreements arose, he was perfectly ready to leave mother and sister, and cleave
to his wife—that was to be.

So Geoffrey Ludlow, tossing like a reed upon
the waters, but ever, like the same reed, drifting
with the resistless current of his will, made up
his mind; and all the sage experience of William
Bowker, illustrated by the story of his life, failed
in altering his determination. It is questionable
whether a younger man might not have been
swayed by, or frightened at, the counsel given

to him. Youth is impressible in all ways; and however people may talk of the headstrong passion of youth, it is clear that—nowadays at least—there is a certain amount of selfish forethought mingled with the heat and fervour; that love—like the measles—though innocuous in youth, is very dangerous when taken in middle life; and Geoffrey Ludlow was as weak, and withal as stubborn, an im-patient, as ever caught the disease.

And yet?—and yet?—was the chain so strong, were the links already so well riveted, as to defy every effort to break them? Or, in truth, was it that the effort was wanting? An infatuation for a woman had been painted in very black shadows by William Bowker; but it was a great question to Geoff whether there was not infinite pleasure in the mere fact of being infatuated. Since he had seen Margaret Dacre—at all events, since he had been fascinated by her — not merely was he a different man, so far as she was concerned, but all life was to him a different and infinitely more pleasurable thing. That strange doubting and hesitation which had been his bane through life seemed, if not to have entirely vanished, at all events to be greatly modified; and he had recently, in one or two matters, shown a decision which had astonished the members of his little household. He felt that he had at last—what he had wanted all through his life—a purpose; he felt that there was something for him to live for; that by his love he had learned something that he had never known before; that his soul was opened, and the whole aspect of nature intensified and beautified; that he might have said with Maud's lover in that exquisite poem of the Laureate's, which so few really appreciate—

> " It seems that I am happy, that to me
> A livelier emerald twinkles in the grass,
> A purer sapphire melts into the sea."

Then he sat down at his easel again, and worked away at the Scylla head, which came out grandly, and soon grew all a-glow with Margaret Dacre's peculiar expression; and then, after contemplating it long and lovingly, the desire to see the original came madly upon him, and he threw down his palette and brushes, and went out.

He walked straight to Mrs. Flexor's, and, on his knocking, the door was opened to him by that worthy dame, who announced to him, with awful solemnity, that he'd "find a change up-stairs."

"A change!" cried Geoffrey, his heart thump-ing audibly, and his cheek blanched ; "a change !"

"O, nothin' serious, Mr. Ludlows ; but she have been a worritin' herself, poor lamb, and a cryin' her very eyes out. But what it is I can't make out, though statin' put your trust in one where trust is doo, continual."

"I don't follow you yet, Mrs. Flexor. Your lodger has been in low spirits—is that it ?"

"Sperrits isn't the name for it, Mr. Ludlows, when downer than dumps is what one would ex-press. As queer as Dick's hatband have she been ever since you went away yesterday; and I says to her at tea last evening—"

"I can see her, I suppose ?"

"Of course you can, sir ; which all I was doing was to prepare you for the—" but here Mrs. Flexor, who had apparently taken something stronger than usual with her dinner, broke down and became inarticulate.

Geoffrey pushed past her, and, knooking at the parlour-door, entered at once. He found Margaret standing, with her arms on the mantelshelf, surveying herself in the wretched little scrap of looking-glass which adorned the wall. Her hair was arranged in two large full bands, her eyes were swollen, and her face was blurred and marked by tears. She did not turn round at the opening of the door, nor, indeed, until she had raised her head and seen in the glass Geoff's reflection ; even then she moved languidly, as though in pain, and her hand, when she placed it in his, was dry with burning heat.

"That chattering idiot down stairs was right, after all," said Geoff, looking alarmedly at her ; " you are ill ?"

"No," she said, with a faint smile ; " not ill, at all events not now. I have been rather weak and silly ; but I did not expect you yet. I intended to remove all traces of such folly by the time you came. It was fit I should, as

I want to talk to you most seriously and so-
berly."

"Do we not always talk so? did we not the
last time I was here—yesterday?"

"Well, generally, perhaps; but not the last
time—not yesterday. If I could have thought so,
I should have spared myself a night of agony and
a morning of remorse."

Geoff's face grew clouded.

"I am sorry for your agony, but much more
sorry for your remorse, Miss Dacre," said he.

"Ah, Mr. Ludlow," cried Margaret passionately, "don't *you* be angry with me; don't *you*
speak to me harshly, or I shall give way altogether!
O, I watched every change of your face; and I
saw what you thought at once; but indeed, indeed
it is not so. My remorse is not for having told
you all that I did yesterday; for what else could I
do to you who had been to me what you had? My
remorse was for what I had done—not for what I
had said—for the wretched folly which prompted
me to yield to a wheedling tongue, and so ruin
myself for ever."

Her tears burst forth again as she said this, and she stamped her foot upon the ground.

" Ruin you tor ever, Margaret!" said Geoffrey, stealing his arm round her waist as she still stood by the mantelshelf; " O no, not ruin you, dearest Margaret—"

" Ah, Mr. Ludlow," she interrupted, neither withdrawing from nor yielding to his arm, " have I not reason to say ruin ? Can I fail to see that you have taken an interest in me which—which—"

" Which nothing you have told me can alter— which I shall preserve, please God," said Geoff, in all simplicity and sincerity, " to the end of my life."

She looked at him as he said these words with a fixed regard, half of wonder, half of real unfeigned earnest admiration.

" I—I'm a very bad hand at talking, Margaret, and know I ought to say a great deal for which I can't find words. You see," he continued with a grave smile, " I'm not a young man now, and I suppose one finds it more difficult to express oneself about—about such matters. But

I'm going to ask you—to—to share my lot—to be my wife !"

Her heart gave one great bound within her breast, and her face was paler than ever, as she said :

" Your wife ! your wife ! Do you know what you are saying, Mr. Ludlow? or is it I who, as the worldling, must point out to you—"

" I know all," said Geoffrey, raising his hand deprecatingly; but she would not be silenced.

" I must point out to you what you would bring upon yourself—what you would have to endure. The story of my life is known to you, and to you alone; not another living soul has ever heard it. My mother died while I was in Italy ; and of—the other person—nothing has ever been heard since his flight. So far, then, I do not fear that my—my shame—we will use the accepted term —would be flung in your teeth, or that you would be made to wince under any thing that might be said about me. But you would know the facts yourself; you could not hide them from your own heart; they would be ever present to you ; and in introducing me to your friends, your relatives,. if you have any, you would feel that—"

"I don't think we need go into that, Margaret. I see how right and how honourable are your motives for saying all this; but I have thought it over, and do not attach one grain of importance to it. If you say 'yes' to me, we shall live for ourselves, and with a very few friends who will appreciate us for ourselves. Ah, I was going to say that to you. I'm not rich, Margaret, and your life would, I'm afraid, be dull. A small income and a small house, and—"

"It would be my home, and I should have you;" and for the first time during the interview she gave him one of her long dreamy looks out of her half-shut eyes.

"Then you will say 'yes,' dearest?" asked Geoff passionately.

"Ah, how can I refuse! how can I deny myself such happiness as you hold out to me after the misery I have gone through!"

"Ah, darling, you shall forget that—"

"But you must not act rashly—must not do

in a moment what you would repent your life
long. Take a week for consideration. Go over
every thing in your mind, and then come back
to me and tell me the result."

" I know it now. O, don't hesitate, Margaret;
don't let me wait the horrid week !"

" It is right, and so we will do it. It will
be more tedious to me than to you, my—my
Geoffrey."

Ah, how caressingly she spoke, and what a
look of love and passion glowed in her deep-
violet eyes!

" And I am not to see you during this week ?"

" No; you shall be free from whatever little
influence my presence may possess. You shall
go now. Good-bye."

" God bless you, my darling !" He bent down
and kissed her upturned mouth, then was gone.
She looked after him wistfully; then after some
time said softly to herself: " I did not believe
there lived so good a man."

CHAPTER XII.

MR. BOWKER was not the only one of Geoffrey
Ludlow's friends to whom that gentleman's inten-
tions towards the lodger at Flexor's occasioned
much troubled thought. Charley Potts regarded
his friend's intimacy in that quarter with any
thing but satisfaction; and an enormous amount
of bird's-eye tobacco was consumed by that rising
young artist in solemn cogitation over what was
best to be done in the matter. For though
Geoffrey had reposed no confidence in his friend,
and, indeed, had never called upon him, and
abstained as much as possible from meeting
him since the night of the adventure outside the
Titian Sketching-Club, yet Mr. Potts was pretty
accurately informed of the state of affairs, through
the medium of Mr. Flexor, then perpetually

sitting for the final touches to Gil Blas; and having a tolerable acquaintance with human nature, —or being, as he metaphorically expressed it, "able to reckon how many blue beans made five," —Mr. Potts was enabled to arrive at a pretty accurate idea of how affairs stood in Little Flotsam Street. And affairs, as they existed in Little Flotsam Street, were by no means satisfactory to Mr. Charles Potts. Had it been a year ago, he would have cared but little about it. A man of the world, accustomed to take things as they were, without the remotest idea of ever setting himself up to · correct abuses, or protest against a habitude of being not strictly in accordance with the views of the most strait-laced, Charley Potts had floated down the stream of life, objecting to nothing, objected to by none. There were fifty ladies of his acquaintance, passing as the wives of fifty men of his acquaintance, pleasant genial creatures, capital punch-mixers,—women in whose presence you might wear your hat, smoke, talk slang, chaff, and sing; women who knew all the art-gossip, and entered into it; whom one could take to the Derby, or who would be delighted with a cheap-veal-and-ham-pie, beer-in-a-stone-jar, and bottle-of-hot-sherry picnic in Bushey Park, — the copy of whose marriage-licenses Charley never expected to see. It was nothing to him, he used to say. It might or it might not be; but he didn't think that Joe's punch would be any the stronger, or Tom's weeds any the better, or Bill's barytone voice one atom more tuneful and chirpy, if the Archbishop of Canterbury had given out the bans and performed the ceremony for the lot. There was in it, he thought, a glorious phase of the *vie de Bohême*, a scorn of the respectable conventionalities of so-ciety, a freedom of thought and action possessing a peculiar charm of their own; and he looked upon the persons who married and settled, and paid taxes and tradesmen's bills, and had children, and went to bed before morning, and didn't smoke clay pipes and sit in their shirt-sleeves, with that softened pity with which the man bound for Epsom Downs regards the City-clerk going to business on the Clapham omnibus.

But within the last few months Mr. Potts's ideas had very considerably changed. It was not because he had attained the venerable age of thirty, though he was at first inclined to ascribe the alteration to that; it was not that his appetite for fun and pleasure had lost any of its keenness, nor that he had become "awakened," or "enlightened," or subjected to any of the preposterous revival influences of the day. It was simply that he had, in the course of his intimacy with Geoffrey Ludlow, seen a great deal of Geoffrey Ludlow's sister, Til; and that the result of his acquaintance with that young lady was the entire change of his ideas on various most important points. It was astonishing, its effect on him: how, after an evening at Mrs. Ludlow's tea-table—presided over, of course, by Miss Til—Charley Potts, going somewhere out to supper among his old set, suddenly had his eyes opened to Louie's blackened eyelids and Bella's painted cheeks; how Georgie's *h*-slips smote with tenfold horror on his ear, and Carry's cigarette-smoking made him wince with disgust. He had

seen all these things before, and rather liked
them; it was the contrast that induced the new
feeling. Ah, those preachers and pedants,—well-
meaning, right-thinking men,—how utterly futile
are the means which they use for compassing
their ends! In these sceptical times, their pul-
pit denunciations, their frightful stories of wrath
to come, are received with polite shoulder-shrugs
and grins of incredulity; their twopence coloured
pictures of the Scarlet Woman, their time-worn
renderings of the street-wanderer, are sneered at
as utterly fictitious and untrue; and meanwhile
detached villas in St. John's Wood, and first-floors
in quiet Pimlico streets, command the most preposterous rents. Young men will of course be young
men; but the period of young-man-ism in that
sense narrows and contracts every year. The
ranks of her Scarlet Ladyship's army are now
filled with very young boys who do not know
any better, or elderly men who cannot get into
the new groove, and who still think that to be
gentlemanly it is necessary to be immoral. Those
writers who complain of the "levelling" tone of

society, and the "fast" manners of our young
ladies, scarcely reflect upon the improved morality
of the age. Our girls—all the outcry about fast-
ness and selling themselves for money notwithstanding—are as good and as domestic as when
formed under the literary auspices of Mrs. Cha-
pone; and—granting the existence of Casinos
and Anonymas—our young men are infinitely
more wholesome than the class for whose instruc-
tion Philip Dormer Stanhope, Earl of Chester-
field, penned his delicious letters.

So Mr. Charles Potts, glowing with newly-
awakened ideas of respectability, began to think
that, after all, the *vie de Bohême* was perhaps a
mistake, and not equal, in the average amount of
happiness derived from it, to the *vie de* Camden
Town. He began to think that to pay rent and
taxes and tradesmen's bills was very likely no
dearer, and certainly more satisfactory, than to
invest in pensions for cast-off mistresses and pro-
visions for illegitimate children. He began to
think, in fact, that a snug little house in the
suburbs, with his own Lares and Penates about

him, and Miss Matilda Ludlow, now looking over
his shoulder and encouraging him at his work,
now confronting him at the domestic dinner-table,
was about the pleasantest thing which his fancy
could conjure up in his then frame of mind.

Thinking all this, devoutly hoping it might so
fall out, and being, like most converts, infinitely
more rabid in the cause of Virtue than those who
had served her with tolerable fidelity for a series
of years, Mr. Charley Potts heard with a dreadful amount of alarm and amazement of Geoffrey
Ludlow's close connection with a person whose
antecedents were not comeatable and siftable by a
local committee of Grundys. A year ago, and
Charley would have laughed the whole business
to scorn; insisted that every man had a right to
do as he liked; slashed at the doubters; mocked
their shaking heads and raised shoulders; and
taken no heed of any thing that might have been
said. But matters were different now. Not
merely was Charley a recruit in the Grundy ranks,
having pinned the Grundy colours in his coat,
and subscribed to the Grundy oath; but the

person about to be brought before the Grundy
Fehmgericht, or court-marshal, was one in whom,
should his hopes be realised, he would have the
greatest interest. Though he had never dared to
express his hopes, though he had not the smallest
actual foundation for his little air-castle, Charles
Potts naturally and honestly regarded Matilda Ludlow as the purest and most honourable of her sex—
as does every young fellow regard the girl he
loves; and the idea that she should be associated,
or intimately connected, with any one under a
moral taint, was to him terrible and loathsome.

The moral taint, mind, was all hypothetical.
Charles Potts had not heard one syllable of Margaret Dacre's history, had been told nothing about
it, knew nothing of her except that he and Geoffrey had saved her from starvation in the streets.
But when people go in for the public profession
of virtue, it is astonishing to find how quickly
they listen to reports of the shortcomings and
backslidings of those who are not professedly in
the same category. It seemed a bit of fatalism
too, that this acquaintance should have occurred

immediately on Geoffrey's selling his picture for a large sum to Mr. Stompff. Had he not done this, there is no doubt that the other thing would have been heard of by few, noticed by none; but in art, as in literature, and indeed in most other professions, no crime is so heavily visited as that of being successful. It is the sale of your picture, or the success of your novel, that first makes people find out how you steal from other people, how your characters are mere reproductions of your own personal friends,—for which you ought to be shunned,—how laboured is your pathos, and how poor your jokes. It is the repetition of your success that induces the criticism; not merely that you are a singular instance of the badness of the public taste, but that you have a red nose, a decided cast in one eye, and that undoubtedly your grandmother had hard labour for stealing a clock. Geoff Ludlow the struggling might have done as he liked without comment; on Geoff Ludlow the possessor of unlimited commissions from the great Stompff it was meet that every vial of virtuous wrath should be poured.

Although Charles Potts knew the loquacity of
Mr. Flexor,—the story of Geoff's adventure and
fascination had gone the round of the studios,—
he did not think how much of what had occurred,
or what was likely to occur, was actually known,
inasmuch as that most men, knowing the close intimacy existing between him and Ludlow, had the
decency to hold their tongues in his presence.
But one day he heard a good deal more than
every thing. He was painting on a fancy head
which he called "Diana Vernon," but which, in
truth, was merely a portrait of Miss Matilda Ludlow very slightly idealised (the " Gil Blas " had
been sent for acceptance or rejection by the Academy Committee), and Bowker was sitting by
smoking a sympathetic pipe, when there came a
sharp tug at the bell, and Bowker, getting up to
open the door, returned with a very rueful coun-
tenance, closely followed by little Tidd. Now
little Tidd, though small in stature, was a great
ruffian. A soured, disappointed little wretch himself, he made it the business of his life to go about
maligning every one who was successful, and

endeavouring, when he came across them personally, to put them out of conceit by hints and innuendoes. He was a nasty-looking little man, with an always grimy face and hands, a bald head, and a frizzled beard. He had a great savage mouth with yellow tusks at either end of it; and he gave you, generally, the sort of notion of a man that you would rather not drink after. He had been contemporary with Geoffrey Ludlow at the Academy, and had been used to say very frankly to him and others, "When I become a great man, as I'm sure to do, I shall cut all you chaps;" and he meant it. But years had passed, and Tidd had not become a great man yet; on the contrary, he had subsided from yards of high-art canvas into portrait-painting, and at that he seemed likely to remain.

"Well, how do *you* do, Potts?" said Mr. Tidd. "I said 'How do you do?' to our friend Mr. Bowker at the door. Looks well, don't he? His troubles seem to sit lightly on him." Here Mr. Bowker growled a bad word, and seemed as if about to spring upon the speaker.

"And what's this you're doing, Potts? A charming head! a charming—n-no! not quite so charming when you get close to it! nose a little out of drawing, and—rather spotty, eh? What do you say, Mr. Bowker?"

"I say, Mr. Tidd, that if you could paint like that, you'd give one of your ears."

"Ah, yes—well, that's not complimentary, but—soured, poor man; sad affair! Yes, well! You've sent your Gil Blas to the Academy, I suppose, Potts?"

"O, yes; he's there, sir; very likely at this moment being held up by a carpenter before the Fatal Three."

"Ah! don't be surprised at its being kicked out."

"I don't intend to be."

"That's right; they're sending them back in shoals this year, I'm told—in shoals. Have you heard any thing about the pictures?"

"Nothing, except that Landseer's got something stunning."

"Landseer, ah!" said Mr. Tidd. "When I

think of that man, and the prices he gets, my
blood boils, sir—boils! That the British public
should care about and pay for a lot of stupid
horses and cattle-pieces, and be indifferent to real
art, is—well, never mind!" and Mr. Tidd gave
himself a great blow in the chest, and asked,
" What else ?"

" Nothing else—O yes! I heard from Rush-
worth, who's on the Council, you know, that they
had been tremendously struck by Geoff Ludlow's
pictures, and that one or two more of the same
sort are safe to make him an Associate."

" What!" said Mr. Tidd, eagerly biting his
nails. " What!—an Associate! Geoffrey Ludlow an Associate!"

" Ah, that seems strange to you, don't it,
Tidd?" said Bowker, speaking for the first time.
" I recollect you and Geoff together drawing from
the life. You were going to do every thing in
those days, Tidd; and old Geoff was as quiet and
as modest as—as he is now. It's the old case of
the hare and the tortoise; and you're the hare,
Tidd;—though, to look at you," added Mr. Bow-

ker under his breath, " you're a d—d sight more like the tortoise, by Jove !"

" Geoffrey Ludlow an Associate!" repeated Mr. Tidd, ignoring Mr. Bowker's remark, and still greedily biting his nails. " Well, I should hardly have thought that; though you can't tell what they won't do down in that infernal place in Trafalgar Square. They've treated me badly enough; and it's quite like them to make a pet of him."

" How have they treated you badly, Tidd?" asked Potts, in the hope of turning the conversation away from Ludlow and his doings.

" How!" screamed Tidd; " in a thousand ways! They've a personal hatred of me, sir— that's what they have ! I've tried every dodge and painted in every school, and they won't have me. The year after Smith made a hit with that miserable picture ' Measuring Heights,' from the *Vicar of Wakefield*, I sent in ' Mr. Burchell cries Fudge !'—kicked out ! The year after, Mr. Ford got great praise for his wretched daub of ' Dr. Johnson reading Goldsmith's Manuscript.' I sent in 'Goldsmith, Johnson, and Bozzy at the Mitre Tavern'—kicked out!—a glorious bit of humour, in which I'd represented all three in different stages of drunkenness—kicked out!"

" I suppose you've not been used worse than most of us, Tidd," growled Mr. Bowker. " She's an unjust stepmother, is the R.A. of A. But she snubs pretty nearly every body alike."

" Not at all!" said Tidd. " Here's this Ludlow—"

" What of him?" interposed Potts quickly.

" Can any one say that his painting is—ah, well! poor devil! it's no good saying any thing more about him; he'll have quite enough to bear on his own shoulders soon."

" What, when he's an Associate?" said Bowker, who inwardly was highly delighted at Tidd's evident rage.

" Associate! —stuff! I mean when he's married."

" Married? Is Ludlow going to be married?"

" Of course he is. Haven't you heard it? it's all over town." And indeed it would have been strange if the story had not permeated all those parts of the town which Mr. Tidd visited, as he himself had laboured energetically for its circulation. " It's all over town—O, a horrible thing! horrible thing!"

Bowker looked across at Charley Potts, who said, " What do you mean by a horrible thing, Tidd? Speak out and tell us; don't be hinting in that way."

" Well, then, Ludlow's going to marry some dreadful bad woman. O, it's a fact; I know all about it. Ludlow was coming home from a dinner-party one night, and he saw this woman, who was drunk, nearly run over by an omnibus at the Regent Circus. He rushed into the road, and pulled her out; and finding she was so drunk she couldn't speak, he got a room for her at Flexor's, and took her there, and has been to see her every day since; and at last he's so madly in love with her that he's going to marry her."

" Ah!" said Mr. Bowker; " who is she? Where did she come from?"

" Nobody knows where she came from; but

she's a reg'lar bad 'un,—as common as dirt.
Pity too, ain't it? for I've heard Ludlow's mother
is a nice old lady, and I've seen his sister, who's
stunnin'!" and Mr. Tidd winked his eye.

This last proceeding finished Charley Potts,
and caused his wrath, which had been long sim-
mering, to boil over. " Look here, Mr. Tidd!"
he burst forth; "that story about Geoff Ludlow
is all lies—all lies, do you hear! And if I find
that you're going about spreading it, or if you
ever mention Miss Ludlow as you did just now,
I'll break your infernal neck for you!"

" Mr. Potts!" said Tidd,—" Mr. Potts, such
language! Mr. Bowker, did you hear what he
said?"

" I did," growled old Bowker over his pipe;
"and from what I know of him, I should think
he was deuced likely to do it."

Mr. Tidd seemed to be of the same opinion,
for he moved towards the door, and slunk out,
muttering ominously.

" There's a scoundrel for you!" said Charley,
when the door shut behind the retreating Tidd;

"there's a ruffian for you! I've not the least doubt that vagabond got a sort of foundation smattering from that blabbing Flexor, and invented all that about the omnibus and the drunken state and the rest of it himself. If that story gets noised about, it will do Geoff harm."

"Of course it will," said Bowker; "and that's just what Tidd wants. However, I think your threat of breaking his neck has stopped that little brute's tongue. There are some fellows, by Jove! who'll go on lying and libelling you, and who are only checked by the idea of getting a licking, when they shut up like telescopes. I don't know what's to be done about Geoff. He seems thoroughly determined and infatuated."

"I can't understand it."

"*I* can," said old Bowker sadly; "if she's any thing like the head he's painted in his second picture—and I think from his manner it must be deuced like her—I can understand a man's doing any thing for such a woman. Did she strike you as being very lovely?"

"I couldn't see much of her that night, and

she was deadly white and ill; but I didn't think her as good-looking as—some that I know."

"Geoff ought to know about this story that's afloat."

"I think he ought," said Charley. "I'll walk up to his place in a day or two, and see him about it."

"See *him?*" said Bowker. "Ah, all right! Yesterday was not your William's natal day."

CHAPTER XIII.

THE grand epoch of the artistic year had arrived; the tremendous Fehmgericht—appointed to decide on the merits of some hundreds of struggling men, to stamp their efforts with approval or to blight them with rejection—had issued their sentence. The Hanging-Committee had gone through their labours and eaten their dinners; every inch of space on the walls in Trafalgar Square was duly covered; the successful men had received intimation of the "varnishing day," and to the rejected had been despatched a comforting missive, stating that the amount of space at the command of the Academy was so small, that, sooner than place their works in an objectionable position, the Council had determined to ask for their withdrawal. Out of this ordeal Geoffrey Ludlow

had come splendidly. There had always been a
notion that he would "do something;" but he
had delayed so long—near the mark, but never
reaching it—that the original belief in his talents
had nearly faded out. Now, when realisation
came, it came with tenfold force. The old boys
—men of accepted name and fame—rejoiced with
extra delight in his success because it was one in
their own line, and without any giving in to the
doctrines of the new school, which they hated
with all their hearts. They liked the " Sic vos
non vobis" best (for Geoffrey had sternly held to
his title, and refused all Mr. Stompff's entreaties
to give it a more popular character); they looked
upon it, as a more thoroughly legitimate piece
of work. They allowed the excellences of the
" Scylla and Charybdis," and, indeed, some of
them were honest enough to prefer it, as a bit
of real excellence in painting; but others objected
to the pre-Raphaelite tendency to exalt the white
face and the dead-gold hair into a realisation
of beauty. But all were agreed that Geoffrey
Ludlow had taken the grand step which was

always anticipated from him, and that he was, out and away, the most promising man of the day. So Geoff was hung on the line, and received letters from half-a-dozen great names congratulating him on his success, and was in the seventh heaven of happiness, principally from the fact that in all this he saw a prospect of excellent revenue, of the acquisition of money and honour to be shared with a person then resident in Mr. Flexor's lodgings, soon to be mistress of his own home.

The kind Fates had also been propitious to Mr. Charles Potts, whose picture of " Gil Blas and the Archbishop" had been well placed in the North Room. Mr. Tidd's " Boadicea ,. in her Chariot," ten feet by six, had been rejected ; but his portrait of W. Bagglehole, Esq., vestry-clerk of St. Wabash, Little Britain, looked down from the ceiling of the large room and terrified the beholders.

So at length arrived that grand day of the year to the Academicians, when they bid certain privileged persons to the private view of the pictures previous to their public exhibition. The *profanum vulgus*, who are odi'd and arceo'd, pine in vain hope of obtaining a ticket for this great occasion. The public press, the members of the Legislature carefully sifted, a set of old dowagers who never bought a sketch, and who scarcely know a picture from a pipkin, and a few distinguished artists, — these are the happy persons who ere invited to enter the sacred precincts on this eventful day. Geoffrey Ludlow never had been inside the walls on such an occasion—never expected to be : but on the evening before, as he was sitting in his studio smoking a pipe, and thinking that within twenty-four hours he would have Margaret's final decision, looking back over his short acquaintance with her in wonder, looking forward to his future life with her in hope, when a mail-phaeton dashed up to the door, and in the strident tones, " Catch hold, young 'un," shouted to the groom, Geoff recognised the voice of Mr. Stompff, and looking out saw that great capitalist descending from the vehicle.

" Hallo, Ludlow !" said Mr. Stompff, entering the studio ; " how are you ? Quiet pipe after the

day's grind? That's your sort! What will I take,
you were going to say? Well, I think a little
drop of sherry, if you've got it pale and dry,—
as, being a man of taste, of course you have.
Well, those duffers at the Academy have hung you
well, you see! Of course they have. You know
how that's done, of course?"

"I had hoped that the — " Geoff began to
stutter directly it became a personal question with
him—"that the—I was going to say that the pictures were good enough to—"

"'Pictures good enough!'—all stuff! pickles!
The pictures are good—no use in denying that,
and it would be deuced stupid in me, who've
bought 'em! But that's not why they're so well
hung. My men all on the Hanging - Committee—*twiggez-vous?* Last year there were two of
Caniche's men, and a horrible fellow who paints
religious dodges, which no one buys : not one of
my men on the line, and half of them turned out!
I determined to set that right this year, and I've
done it. Just you look where Caniche's men are
to-morrow, that's all!"

" To-morrow ?"

" O, ah! that's what brought me here ; I forgot to tell you. Here's a ticket for the private view. I think you ought to be there,—show yourself, you know, and that kind of thing. And look here : if you see me pointing you out to people, don't you be offended. I've lived longer in the world than you, and I know what's what. Besides, you're part of my establishment just now, and I know the way to work the oracle. So don't mind it, that's all. Very decent glass of sherry, Ludlow ! I say—excuse me, but if you *could* wear a white waistcoat to-morrow, I think I should like it. English gentleman, you know, and all that ! Some of Caniche's fellows are very seedy-looking duffers."

Geoff smiled, took the ticket, and promised to come, terribly uncomfortable at the prospect of notoriety which Mr. Stompff had opened for him. But that worthy had not done with him yet.

" After it's all over," said he, " you must come and dine with me at Blackwall. Regular business of mine, sir. I take down my men and two or

three of the newspaper chaps, after the private
view, and give 'em as good a dinner as money can
buy. No stint! I say to Lovegrove, 'You know
me! The best, and damn the expense!' and Lovegrove does it, and it's all right! It would be
difficult for a fellow to pitch into any of my men
with a recollection of my Moselle about him, and a
hope that it'll come again next year, eh? Well—
won't detain you now; see you to-morrow; and
don't forget the dinner."

Do you not know this kind of man, and does
he not permeate English society?—this coarse
ruffian, whose apparent good-nature disarms your
nascent wrath, and yet whose good-nature you
know to be merely vulgar ostentatious self-asser-
tion under the guise of *bonhomie*. I take the character I have drawn, but I declare he belongs
to all classes. I have seen him as publisher to
author, as attorney to young barrister, as patron
to struggler generally. Geoffrey Ludlow shrank
before him, but shrank in his old feeble hesitating
way; he had not the pluck to shake off the yoke,
and bid his employer go to the devil. It was

a new phase of life for him—a phase which promised competence at a time when competence was
required; which, moreover, rid him of any doubt
or anxiety about the destination of his labour, which
to a man of Ludlow's temperament was all in
all. How many of us are there who will sell such
wares as Providence has given us the power of
producing at a much less rate than we could otherwise obtain for them, and to most objectionable
people, so long as we are enabled to look for and to
get a certain price, and are absorbed from the
ignominy of haggling, even though by that haggling we should be tenfold enriched! So Geoffrey Ludlow took Mr. Stompff's ticket, and gave
him his pale sherry, and promised to dine with
him, and bowed him out; and then went back into
his studio and lit a fresh pipe, and sat down to
think calmly over all that was about to befall him.

What came into his mind first? His love, of
course. There is no man, as yet unanchored in
the calm haven of marriage, who amidst con-
tending perplexities does not first think of what
storms and shoals beset his progress in that

course. And who, so long as there he can see a
bit of blue sky, a tolerably clear passage, does not,
to a great extent, ignore the black clouds which
he sees banking up to windward, the heavy swell
crested with a thin, dangerous, white line of wave,
which threatens his fortunes in another direction.
Here Geoffrey Ludlow thought himself tolerably
secure. Margaret had told him all her story,
had made the worst of it, and had left him to
act on her confession. Did she love him? That
was a difficult question for a man of Geoff's
diffidence to judge. But he thought he might
unhesitatingly answer it in the affirmative. It
was her own proposition that nothing should be
done hurriedly; that he should take the week to
calmly reflect over the position, and see whether
he held by his first avowal. And to-morrow the
week would be at an end, and he would have the
right to ask for her decision.

That decision, if favourable, would at once
settle his plans, and necessitate an immediate
communication to his mother. This was a phase
of the subject which Geoffrey characteristically

had ignored, put by, and refrained from thinking of as long as possible. But now there was no help for it. Under any circumstances he would have endeavoured, on marrying, to set up a separate establishment for himself; but situated as he was, with Margaret Dacre as his intended wife, he saw that such a step was inevitable. For though he loved his mother with all his heart, he was not blind to her weaknesses, and he knew that the " cross" would never be more triumphantly brought forward, or more loudly complained of, than when it took the form of a daughter-in-law,—a daughter-in-law, moreover, whose antecedents were not held up for the old lady's scrutinising inspection. And here, perhaps, was the greatest tribute to the weird influence of the dead-gold hair, the pallid face, and the deep-violet eyes. A year ago, and Geoff Ludlow would have told you that nothing could ever have made him alter his then style of life. It had continued too long, he would have told you; he had settled down into a certain state of routine, living with the old lady and Til: they understood his ways and

wishes, and he thought he should never change.
And Mrs. Ludlow used to say that Geoffrey would
never marry now; he did not care for young
chits of girls, who were all giggle and nonsense,
my dear; a man at his time of life looked for
something more than that, and where it was to
come from she, for one, did not know.   Miss
Matilda had indeed different views on the subject; she thought that dear old Geoff would
marry, but that it would probably come about
in this way.   Some lovely female member of the
aristocracy, to whom Geoff had given drawing-
lessons, or who had seen his pictures, and become
imbued with the spirit of poetry in them, would
say to her father the haughty earl, "I pine for
him; I cannot live without him;" and to save
his darling child's health, the earl would give
his consent, and bestow upon the happy couple
estates of the annual value of twenty thousand
pounds.   But then you see Miss Matilda Ludlow
was given to novel-reading, and though perfectly
practical and unromantic as regards herself and
her career, was apt to look upon all appertaining

to her brother, whom she adored, through a sur-
rounding halo of circulating-library.

How this great intelligence would, then, be
received by his home-tenants set Geoff thinking
after Stompff's departure, and between the puffs
of his pipe he turned the subject hither and
thither in his mind, and proposed to himself all
kinds of ways for meeting the difficulty; none of
which, on reconsideration, appearing practicable
or judicious, he reverted to an old and favourite
plan of his, that of postponing any further deliberation until the next day, when, as he argued with
himself, he would have " slept upon it"—a most
valuable result when the subject is systematically
ignored up to the time of going to sleep, and after
the hour of waking—he would have been to the
private view at the Academy—which had, of
course, an immense deal to do with it—and he
would have received the final decision from Margaret Dacre. O yes, it was useless to think any
more of it that night. And fully persuaded of this,
Geoff turned in and fell fast asleep.

"And there won't be a more gentlemanly-looking man in the rooms than our dear old Geoff!"

"Stuff, Til! don't be absurd!"

"No, I mean it; and you know it too, you vain old thing; else why are you perpetually looking in the glass?"

"No, but—Til, nonsense!—I suppose I'm all right, eh?"

"All right!—you're charming, Geoff! I never saw you such a—I can't help it you know—swell before! Don't frown, Geoff; there's no other word that expresses it. One would think you were going to meet a lady there. Does the Queen go, or any of the young princesses?"

"How can you be so ridiculous, Til! Now, good-bye;" and Geoff gave his sister a hearty kiss, and started off. Miss Matilda was right; he did look perfectly gentlemanly in his dark-blue coat, white waistcoat, and small-check trousers. Nature, which certainly had denied him personal beauty or regularity of feature, had given him two or three marks of distinction: his height, his bright earnest eyes, and a certain indefinable odd expression, different from the ordinary ruck of people—an expression which attracted attention, and invariably made people ask who he was.

It was three o'clock before Geoff arrived at the Academy, and the rooms were crowded. The scene was new to him, and he stared round in astonishment at the brilliancy of the *toilettes*, and what Charley Potts would have called the "air of swelldom" which pervaded the place. It is scarcely necessary to say that his first act was to glance at the Catalogue to see where his pictures were placed; his second, to proceed to them to see how they looked on the walls. Round each was a little host of eager inspectors, and from what Geoff caught of their conversation, the verdict was entirely favourable. But he was not long left in doubt. As he was looking on, his arm was seized by Mr. Stompff, who, scarcely waiting to carry him out of earshot, began, "Well! you've done it up brown this time, my man, and no flies! Your pictures have woke 'em up. They're talking of nothing else. I've sold 'em both. Lord Everton

—that's him over there : little man with a double eyeglass, brown coat and high velvet collar—he's bought the ' Sic wos ;' and Mr. Shirtings of Manchester's got the other. The price has been good, sir ; I'm not above denyin' it. There's six dozen of Sham ready to go into your cellar whenever you say the word : I ain't mean with my men like some people. Power of nobs here to-day. There's the Prime-Minister, and the Chancellor of the Exchequer—that's him in the dirty white hat and rumpled coat—and no end of bishops and old ladies of title. That's Shirtings, that fat man in the black satin waistcoat. Wonderful man, sir,— factory-boy in Manchester ! Saved his shillin' a-week, and is now worth two hundred thousand. Fine modern collection he's got ! That little man in the turn-down collar, with the gold pencil-case in his hand, is Scrunch, the art-critic of the *Scourge.* A bitter little beast ; but I've squared him. I gave him five-and-twenty pounds to write a short account of the Punic War, which was given away with Bliff's picture of ' Regulus,' and he's never pitched into any of my people since.

He's comin' to dinner to-day. O, by the bye, don't be late! I'll drive you down."

"Thank you," said Geoff; "I—I've got somewhere to go to. I'll find my own way to Blackwall."

"Ha!" said Stompff, "then it is true, is it? Never mind; mum's the word! I'm tiled! Look here: don't you mind me if you see me doing anything particular. It's all good for business."

It may have been so, but it was undoubtedly trying. During the next two hours Geoff was conscious of Mr. Stompff's perpetually hovering round him, always acting as cicerone to some different man, to whom he would point out Geoff with his forefinger, then whisper in his companion's ear, indicate one of Geoff's pictures with his elbow, and finish by promenading his friend just under Geoff's nose; the stranger making a feeble pretence of looking at some highly-hung portrait, but obviously swallowing Geoff with his eyes, from his hair to his boots.

But he had also far more pleasurable experiences of his success. Three or four of the leading members of the Academy, men of world-wide fame, whom he had known by sight, and envied— so far as envy lay in his gentle disposition— for years, came up to him, and introducing themselves, spoke warmly of his picture, and complimented him in most flattering terms. By one of these, the greatest of them all, Lord Everton was subsequently brought up; and the kind old man, with that courtesy which belongs only to the highest breeding, shook hands with him, and expressed his delight at being the fortunate possessor of Mr. Ludlow's admirable picture, and hoped to have the pleasure of receiving him at Everton house, and showing him the gallery of old masters, in whose footsteps he, Mr. Ludlow, was so swiftly following.

And then, as Geoffrey was bowing his acknowledgments, he heard his name pronounced, and turning round found himself close by Lord Caterham's wheel-chair, and had a hearty greeting from its occupant.

"How do you do, Mr. Ludlow? You will recollect meeting me at Lady Lilford's, I daresay.

I have just been looking at your pictures, and I congratulate you most earnestly upon them. No, I never flatter. They appear to me very remarkable things, especially the evening-party scene, where you seem to have given an actual spirit of motion to the dancers in the background, so different from the ordinary stiff and angular representation.—You can leave the chair here for a minute, Stephens.—In such a crowd as this, Mr. Ludlow, it's refreshing—is it not?—to get a long look at that sheltered pool surrounded by waving trees, which Creswick has painted so charmingly. The young lady who came with me has gone roving away to search for some favourite, whose name she saw in the Catalogue; but if you don't mind waiting with me a minute, she will be back, and I know she will be glad to see you, as—ah! here she is!"

As Geoffrey looked round, a tall young lady with brown eyes, a pert inquisitive nose, an undulating figure, and a bright laughing mouth, came hurriedly up, and without noticing Geoffrey, bent over Lord Caterham's chair, and said, " I was quite right, Arthur; it is—" then, in obedience to a glance from her companion, she looked up and exclaimed, "What, Geoffrey!—Mr. Ludlow, I mean—O, how *do* you do? Why, you don't mean to say you don't recollect me?"

Geoff was a bad courtier at any time, and now the expression of his face at the warmth of this salutation showed how utterly he was puzzled.

" You *have* forgotten, then? And you don't recollect those days when—"

"Stop!" he exclaimed, a sudden light breaking upon him; "little Annie Maurice that used to live at Willesden Priory! My little fairy, that I have sketched a thousand times. Well, I ought not to have forgotten you, Miss Maurice, for I have studied your features often enough to have impressed them on my memory. But how could I recognise my little elf in such a dashing young lady?"

Lord Caterham looked up at them out of the corners of his eyes as they stood warmly shaking hands, and for a moment his face wore a pained expression; but it passed away directly, and his voice was as cheery as usual as he said, "*Et nos mutamur in illis*, eh, Mr. Ludlow? Little fays grow into dashing young ladies, and indolent young sketchers become the favourites of the Academy."

" Ay," said Annie; "and the dear old Priory let to other people, and many of those who made those times so pleasant are dead and gone. O, Geoffrey—Mr. Ludlow, I mean—"

" Yes," said Geoff, interrupting her; "and Geoffrey turned into Mr. Ludlow, and Annie into Miss Maurice! there's another result of the flight of time, and one which I, for my part, heartily object to."

"Ah, but, Mr. Ludlow, I must bespeak a proper amount of veneration for you on the part of this young lady," said Lord Caterham; "for I am about to ask you to do me a personal favour in which she is involved."

Geoff bowed absently; he was already thinking it was time for him to go to Margaret.

" Miss Maurice is good enough to stay with my family for the present, Mr. Ludlow; and I am very anxious that she should avail herself of the opportunity of cultivating a talent for drawing which she undoubtedly possesses.",

"She used to sketch very nicely years ago," said Geoff, turning to her with a smile; and her face was radiant with good humour as she said:

"O, Geoffrey, do you recollect my attempts at cows?"

"So, in order to give her this chance, and in the hope of making her attempt at cows more creditable than it seems they used to be, I am going to ask you, Mr. Ludlow, to undertake Miss Maurice's artistic education, to give her as much of your time as you can spare, and, in fact, to give what I think I may call her genius the right inclination."

Geoffrey hesitated of course—it was his normal state—and he said doubtingly: "You're very good; but I—I'm almost afraid—"

"You are not bashful, I trust, Mr. Ludlow," said Lord Caterham; "I have seen plenty of your work at Lady Lilford's, and I know you to be perfectly competent."

"It was scarcely that, my lord; I rather think that—" but when he got thus far he looked up and saw Annie Maurice's brown eyes lifted to his in such an appealing glance that he finished his sentence by saying: "Well, I shall be very happy indeed to do all that I can—for old acquaintance-sake, Annie;" and he held out his hand frankly to her.

"You are both very good," she said; "and it will be a real pleasure to me to re-commence my lessons, and to try to prove to you, Geoffrey, that I'm not so impatient or so stupid as I was. When shall we begin?"

"The sooner the better, don't you think, Mr. Ludlow?" said Lord Caterham.

Geoff felt his face flush as he said: "I—I expect to be going out of town for a week or two; but when I return I shall be delighted to commence."

"When you return we shall be delighted to see you. I can fully understand how you long for a little rest and change after your hard work, Mr. Ludlow. Now, good-bye to you; I hope

this is but the beginning of an intimate acquaintance." And Lord Caterham, nodding to Geoffrey, called Stephens and was wheeled away.

"I like that man, Annie," said he when they
were out of earshot; "he has a thoroughly good
face, and the truth and honesty of his eyes over-
balance the weakness of the mouth, which is undecided, but not shifty. His manner is honest,
too ; don't you think so ?"

He waited an instant for an answer, but
Annie did not speak.

"Didn't you hear me, Annie? or am I not
worth a reply?"

"I—I beg your pardon, Arthur. I heard you
perfectly; but I was thinking. O yes, I should
think Mr. Ludlow was as honest as the day."

"But what made you *distraite?* What were
you thinking of?"

"I was thinking what a wonderful difference
a few years made. I was thinking of my old
ideas of Mr. Ludlow when he used to come out
to dine with papa, and sleep at our house; how
he had long dark hair, which he used to toss off

his face, and poor papa used to laugh at him and call him an enthusiast. I saw hundreds of silver threads in his hair just now, and he seemed— well, I don't know—so much more constrained and conventional than I recollect him."

"You seem to forget that you had frocks and trousers and trundled a hoop in those days, Annie. You were a little fay then; you are a Venus now: in a few years you will be married, and then you must sit to Mr. Ludlow for a Juno. It is only your pretty flowers that change so much; your hollies and yews keep pretty much the same throughout the year."

From the tone of voice in which Lord Caterham made this last remark, Annie knew very well that he was in one of those bitter humours which, when his malady was considered, came surprisingly seldom upon him, and she knew that a reply would only have aggravated his temper, so she forbore and walked silently by his side.

No sooner did he find himself free than Geoffrey Ludlow hurried from the Academy, and jumping into a cab, drove off at once to Little

Flotsam Street. Never since Margaret Dacre had been denizened at Flexor's had Geoff approached the neighbourhood without a fluttering at his heart, a sinking of his spirits, a general notion of fright and something about to happen. But now, whether it was that his success at the Academy and the kind words he had had from all his friends had given him courage, it is impossible to say, but he certainly jumped out of the hansom without the faintest feeling of disquietude, and walked hurriedly perhaps, but by no means nervously, up to Flexor's door.

Margaret was in, of course. He found her, the very perfection of neatness, watering some flowers in her window which he had sent her. She had on a tight-fitting cotton dress of a very small pattern, and her hair was neatly braided over her ears. He had seen her look more voluptuous, never more *piquante* and irresistible. She came across the room to him with outstretched hand and raised eyebrows.

"You have come!" she said; "that's good of you, for I scarcely expected you."

Geoff stopped suddenly. "Scarcely expected me! Yet you must know that to-day the week is ended."

"I knew that well enough; but I heard from the woman of the house here that to-day is the private view of the Academy, and I knew how much you would he engaged."

"And did you think that I should suffer any thing to keep me from coming to you to-day?"

She paused a minute, then looked him full in the face. "No; frankly and honestly I did not. I was using conventionalisms and talking society to you. I never will do so again. I knew you would come, and—and I longed for your coming, to tell you my delight at what I hear is your glorious success."

"My greatest triumph is in your appreciation of it," said Geoff. "Having said to you what I did a week ago, you must know perfectly that the end and aim of all I think, of all I undertake, is connected with you. And you must not keep me in suspense, Margaret, please. You must tell me your decision."

" My decision! Now did we not part, at my suggestion, for a week's adjournment, during which you should turn over in your mind certain positions which I had placed before you? And now, the week ended, you ask for my decision! Surely rather I ought to put the question."

"A week ago I said to you, 'Margaret, be my wife.' It was not very romantically put, I confess; but I'm not a very romantic person. You told me to wait a week, to think over all the circumstances of our acquaintance, and to see whether my determination held good. The week is over; I've done all you said; and I've come again to say, Margaret, be my wife."

It was rather a long speech this for Geoff; and as he uttered it, his dear old face glowed with honest fervour.

"You have thoroughly made up your mind, considered every thing, and decided?"

" I have."

" Mind, in telling you the story of my past life, I spoke out freely, regardless of my own feelings and of yours. You owe me an equal candour. You have thought of all?"

"Of all."

"And you still—"

"I still repeat that one demand."

"Then I say 'Yes,' frankly and freely. Geoffrey Ludlow, I will be your wife; and by Heaven's help I will make your life happy, and atone for my past. I—"

And she did not say any more just then, for Geoff stopped her lips with a kiss.

"What *can* have become of Ludlow?" said Mr. Stompff for about the twentieth time, as he came back into the dining-room, after craning over the balcony and looking all round.

"Giving himself airs on account of his success," said genial Mr. Bowie, the art-critic. "I wouldn't wait any longer for him, Stompff."

"I won't," said Stompff. "Dinner!"

The dinner was excellent, the wine good and plentiful, the guests well assorted, and the conversation as racy and salted as it usually is when a

hecatomb of absent friends is duly slaughtered by
the company. Each man said the direst things
he could about his own personal enemies; and
there were but very few cases in which the rest
of the *convives* did not join in chorus. It was
during a pause in this kind of conversation—much
later in the evening, when the windows had been
thrown open, and most of the men were smoking
in the balcony—that little Tommy Smalt, who
had done full justice to the claret, took his
cigar from his mouth, leaned lazily back, and
looking up at the moonlit sky, felt in such a
happy state of repletion and tobacco as to be
momentarily charitable — the which feeling induced him to say:

"I wish Ludlow had been with us!"

"His own fault that he's not," said Mr.
Stompff; "his own fault entirely. However, he's
missed a pleasant evening. I rather think we've
had the pull of him."

Had Geoff missed a pleasant evening? He
thought otherwise. He thought he had never
had such an evening in his life; for the same cold

steel-blue rays of the early spring moon which fell upon the topers in the Blackwall balcony came gleaming in through Mr. Flexor's first-floor window, lighting up a pallid face set in a frame of dead-gold hair and pillowed on Geoffrey Ludlow's breast.

CHAPTER XIV.

THOSE TWAIN ONE FLESH.

So it was a settled thing between Margaret Dacre and Geoffrey Ludlow. She had acceded to his earnest demand—demand thrice repeated—after due consideration and delay, and she was to become his wife forthwith. Indeed, their colloquy on that delicious moonlight evening would have been brought to a conclusion much sooner than it was, had not Geoff stalwartly declared and manfully held to his determination, spite of every protest, not to go until they had settled upon a day on which to be married. He did not see the use of waiting, he said; it would get buzzed about by the Flexors; and all sorts of impertinent remarks and congratulations would be made, which they could very well do without. Of course, as regarded herself, Margaret would want a—what do you call it ?—outfit, *trousseau*, that was the word. But it appeared to him that all he had to do was to give her the money, and all she had to do was to go out and get the things she wanted, and that need not take any time, or hinder them from naming a day—well, let us say in next week. He himself had certain little arrangements to make ; but he could very well get through them all in that time. And what did Margaret say ?

Margaret did not say very much. She had been lying perfectly tranquil in Geoffrey's arms ; a position which, she said, first gave her assurance that her new life had indeed begun. She should be able to realise it more fully, she thought, when she commenced in a home of her own, and in a fresh atmosphere ; and as the prying curiosity of the Flexors daily increased, and as Little Flotsam Street, with its normal pavement of refuse and its high grim house-rows scarcely admitting any light, was an objectionable residence, she could urge no reason for delay. So a day at the end of the ensuing week was fixed upon ; and no sooner had it been finally determined than Geoff,

ooking round at preparations which were absolutely necessary, was amazed at their number and
magnitude.

He should be away a fortnight, he calculated,
perhaps longer; and it was necessary to apprise
the families and the one or two "ladies' colleges"
in which he taught drawing of his absence. He
would also let Stompff know that he would not
find him in his studio during the next few days
(for it was the habit of this great *entrepreneur* to
pay frequent visits to his *protégés*, just to "give
'em a look-up," as he said; but in reality to see
that they were not doing work for any opposition
dealer); but he should simply tell Stompff that
he was going out of town for a little change,
leaving that worthy to imagine that he wanted
rest after his hard work. And then came a point
at which he hitched up at once, and was metaphorically thrown on his beam-ends. What was
he to say to his mother and sister and to his
intimate friends?

To the last, of course, there was no actual
necessity to say any thing, save that he knew he

must have some one to "give away" the bride, and he would have preferred one of his old friends, even at the risk of an explanation, to Flexor, hired for five shillings, and duly got up in the costume of the old English gentleman. But to his mother and sister it was absolutely necessary that some kind of notice should be given. It was necessary they should know that the little household, which, despite various small interruptions, had been carried on so long in amity and affection, would be broken up, so far as he was concerned; also necessary that they should know that his contribution to the household income would remain exactly the same as though he still partook of its benefits. He had to say all this; and he was as frightened as a child. He thought of writing at first, and of leaving a letter to be given to his mother after the ceremony was over; of giving a bare history in a letter, and an amount of affection in the postscript which would melt the stoniest maternal heart. But a little reflection caused him to think better of this notion, and determined him to seek an interview with his mother. It was due to her, and he would go through with it.

So one morning, when he had watched his sister Til safe off into a prolonged diplomatic controversy with the cook, involving the reception of divers ambassadors from the butcher and other tradespeople, Geoff made his way into his mother's room, and found her knitting something which might have been either an antimacassar for a giant or a counterpane for a child, and at once intimated his pleasure at finding her alone, as he had "something to say to her."

This was an ominous beginning in Mrs. Ludlow's ears, and her "cross" at once stood out visibly before her; Constantine himself had never seen it plainer. The mere pronunciation of the phrase made her nervous; she ought to have "dropped one and taken up two;" but her hands got complicated, and she stopped with a knitting-needle in mid-air.

"If you're alluding to the butcher's book, Geoffrey," she said, "I hold myself blameless. It was understood, thoroughly understood that it should be eightpence a pound all round; and if Smithers chooses to charge ninepence-halfpenny for lamb, and you allow it, I don't hold myself responsible. I said to your sister at the time—I said, ' Matilda, I'm sure Geoffrey—' "

" It's not that, mother, I want to talk to you about," said Geoff, with a half-smile ; " it's a bigger subject than the price of butcher's meat. I want to talk to you about myself—about my future life."

" Very well, Geoffrey ; that does not come upon me unawares. I am a woman of the world. I ought to be, considering the time I had with your poor father ; and I suppose that now you're making a name, you'll find it necessary to enter-tain. He did, poor fellow, though it's little enough name or money he ever made ! But if you want to see your friends round you, there must be help in the kitchen. There are certain things— jellies, and that like—that must come from the pastry-cook's ; but all the rest we can do very well at home with a little help in the kit-chen."

"You don't comprehend me yet, mother. I—I'm going to leave you."

"To leave us!—O, to live away! Very well, Geoffrey," said the old lady, bridling up; "if you've grown too grand to live with your mother, I can only say I'm sorry for you. Though I never saw my name in print in the *Times* newspaper, except among the marriages; and if that's to be the effect it has upon me, I hope I never shall."

"My dear mother, how *can* you imagine any thing so absurd! The truth is—"

"O yes, Geoffrey, I understand. I've not lived for sixty years in the world for nothing. Not that there's been ever the least word said about your friends coming pipe-smoking at all times of the night, or hot water required for spirits when Emma was that dead with sleep she could scarcely move; nor about young persons—female models you call them—trolloping misses I say."

It is worthy of remark that in all business matters Mrs. Ludlow was accustomed to treat her son as a cipher, forgetting that two-thirds of the income by which the house was supported were contributed by him. There was no thought of this, however, in honest old Geoff's mind as he said,

" Mother, you won't hear me out! The fact is, I'm going to be married."

" To be married, Geoffrey!" said the old lady, in a voice that was much softer and rather tremulous; " to be married, my dear boy! Well, that is news!" Her hands trembled as she laid them on his big shoulders and put up her face to kiss him. " Well, well, to be sure! I never thought you'd marry now, Geoffrey. I looked upon you as a confirmed old bachelor. And who is it that has caught you at last? Not Miss Sanders, is it?"

Geoffrey shook his head.

" I thought not. No, that would never do. Nice kind of girl too; but if we're to hold our heads so high when all our money comes out of sugar-hogsheads in Thames Street, why where will be the end of it, I should like to know? It isn't Miss Hall?"

Geoffrey repeated his shake.

" Well, I'm glad of it; not but what I'm very fond of Emily Hall; but that half-pay father of hers! I shouldn't like some of the people about here to know that we were related to a half-pay captain with a wooden leg; and he'd be always clumping about the house, and be horrible for the carpets! Well, if it isn't Minnie Beverley, I'll give it up; for you'd never go marrying that tall Dickenson, who's more like a dromedary than a woman!"

" It is not Minnie Beverley, nor the young lady who's like a dromedary," said Geoff, laughing. " The young lady I am going to marry is a stranger to you; you have never even seen her."

" Never seen her! O Geoff!" cried the old lady, with horror in her face, " you're never going to marry one of those trolloping models, and bring her home to live with us?"

" No, no, mother; you need be under no alarm. This young lady, who is from the country, is thoroughly ladylike and well educated. But I shall not bring her home to you; we shall have a house of our own."

"And what shall we do, Til and I? O Geoffrey, I shall never have to go into lodgings at my time of life, shall I, and after having kept house and had my own plate and linen for so many years?"

"Mother, do you imagine I should increase my own happiness at the expense of yours? Of course you'll keep this house, and all arrangements will go on just the same as usual, except that I sha'n't be here to worry you."

"You never worried me, my dear," said the old lady, as all his generosity and noble unselfishness rose before her mind; "you never worried me, but have been always the best of sons; and pray God that you may be happy, for you deserve it." She put her arms round his neck and kissed him fondly, while the tears trickled down her cheeks. "Ah, here's Til," she continued, drying her eyes; "it would never do to let her see me being so silly."

"O, here you are at last!" said Miss Til,

who, as they both noticed, had a very high colour
and was generally suffused about the face and
neck; "what have you been conspiring about?
The Mater looks as guilty as possible, doesn't she,
Geoff? and you're not much better, sir. What
is the matter?"

"I suspect you're simply attempting the au-
thoritative to cover your own confusion, Til.
There's something—"

"No, no! I won't be put off in that manner!
What *is* the matter?"

"There's nothing the matter, my dear," said
Mrs. Ludlow, who by this time had recovered her
composure; "though there is some great news.
Geoffrey's going to be married!"

"What!" exclaimed Miss Til, and then made
one spring into his arms. "O, you darling old
Geoff, you don't say so? O, how quiet you
have kept it, you horrible hypocrite, seeing us
day after day and never breathing a word about
it! Now, who is it, at once? Stop, shall I guess?
Is it any one I know?"

"No one that you know."

" O, I am so glad! Do you know, I think
I hate most people I know—girls, I mean ; and
I'm sure none of them are nice enough for my
Geoff. Now, what's she like, Geoff?"

" O, I don't know."

" That's what men always say—so tiresome!
Is she dark or fair?"

" Well, fair, I suppose."

" And what-coloured hair and eyes?"

" Eh? well, her hair is red, I think."

" Red! Lor, Geoff! what they call carrots?"

" No ; deep-red, like red gold—"

" O, Geoff, I know, I know! Like the Scylla
in the picture. O, you worse than fox, to de-
ceive me in that way, telling me it was a model,
and all the rest of it. Well, if she's like that, she
must be wonderful to look at, and I'm dying to
see her. What's her name?"

" Margaret."

" Margaret! That's very nice; I like Margaret very much. Of course you'll never let
yourself be sufficiently childishly spoony to let it
drop into Peggy, which is atrocious. I'm very

glad she's got a nice name; for, do all I could, I'm certain I never could like a sister-in-law who was called Belinda or Keziah, or any thing dreadful."

"Have you fixed your wedding-day, Geoffrey?"

"Yes, mother; for Thursday next."

"Thursday!" exclaimed Miss Til. "Thursday next? why there'll be no time for me to get any thing ready; for I suppose, as your sister, Geoff, I'm to be one of the bridesmaids?"

"There will be no bridesmaids, dear Til," said Geoffrey; "no company, no breakfast. I have always thought that, if ever I married, I should like to walk into the church with my bride, have the service gone through, and walk out again, without the least attempt at show; and I'm glad to find that Margaret thoroughly coincides with me."

"But surely, Geoffrey," said Mrs. Ludlow, "your friends will—"

"O my! Talking of friends," interrupted Miss Til, "I quite forgot in all this flurry to tell you that Mr. Charles Potts is in the drawing-room, waiting to see you, Geoffrey."

" Dear me! is he indeed? ah, that accounts for a flushed face—"

" Don't be absurd, Geoff! Shall I tell him to come here ?"

" You may if you like; but don't come back with him, as I want five minutes' quiet talk with him."

So Mrs. Ludlow and her daughter left the studio, and in a few minutes Charley Potts arrived. As he walked up to Geoffrey and wrung his hand, both men seemed under some little constraint. Geoff spoke first.

" I'm glad you're here, Charley. I should have gone up to your place if you hadn't looked in to-day. I have something to tell you, and something to ask of you."

" Tell away, old boy; and as for the asking, look upon it as done,—unless it's tin, by the way; and there I'm no good just now."

" Charley, I'm going to be married next Thursday to Margaret Dacre—the girl we found

fainting in the streets that night of the Titians."

Geoff expected some exclamation, but his
friend only nodded his head.

"She has told me her whole life: insisted
upon my hearing it before I said a word to her;
made me wait a week after I had asked her to
be my wife, on the chance that I should repent;
behaved in the noblest way."

Geoffrey again paused, and Mr. Potts again
nodded.

"We shall be married very quietly at the
parish-church here; and there will be nobody
present but you. I want you to come; will
you?"

"Will I? Why, old man, we've been like
brothers for years; and to think that I'd desert
you at a time like this! I—I didn't quite mean
that, you know; but if not, why not? You
know what I do mean."

"Thanks, Charley. One thing more: don't
talk about it until after it's over. I'm an awk-
ward subject for chaff, particularly such chaff as

this would give rise to. You may tell old Bowker, if you like; but no one else."

And Mr. Potts went away without delivering
that tremendous philippic with which he had come
charged. Perhaps it was his conversation with
Miss Til in the drawing-room which had softened
his manners and prevented him from being brutal.

They were married on the following Thursday; Margaret looking perfectly lovely in her
brown-silk dress and white bonnet. Charley
Potts could not believe her to be the haggard
creature in whose rescue he had assisted; and
simple old William Bowker, peering out from
between the curtains of a high pew, was amazed
at her strange weird beauty. The ceremony was
over; and Geoff, happy and proud, was leading
his wife down the steps of the church to the fly
waiting for them, when a procession of carriages,
coachmen and footmen with white favours, and
gaily-clad company, all betokening another wed-
ding, drove up to the door. The bride and her
bridesmaids had alighted, and the bridegroom's

best-man, who with his friend had just jumped out of his cabriolet, was bowing to the bridesmaids as Geoff and Margaret passed. He was a pleasant airy fellow, and seeing a pretty woman coming down the steps, he looked hard at her. Their eyes met, and there was something in Margaret's glance which stopped him in the act of raising his hand to his hat. Geoffrey saw nothing of this; he was waving his hand to Bowker, who was standing by; and they passed on to the fly.

"Come on, Algy!" called out the impatient intended bridegroom; "they'll be waiting for us in the church. What on earth are you staring at?"

"Nothing, dear old boy!" said Algy Barford, who was the best-man just named,—"nothing but a resurrection!—only a resurrection; by Jove, that's all!"

END OF BOOK THE FIRST.

ROBSON AND SON, PRINTERS, PANCRAS ROAD, N.W.

www.ingramcontent.com/pod-product-compliance
Lightning Source LLC
Chambersburg PA
CBHW020854020726
47497CB00005B/1397